Stasha's Cure

To Barb & Steve
Good neighbours make
the best friends

K Rawlland.

ISBN: 1-4196-3375-9

To order additional copies, please contact us.
BookSurge, LLC
www.booksurge.com
1-866-308-6235
orders@booksurge.com

Stasha's Cure

Karen Rouillard

2006

Stasha's Cure

I would like to dedicate this book to my mother.
She has survived cancer twice and has never lost hope.
I love you Mom.

October 17, 1977

She was so small sitting there on the swing in the backyard. She could hear the crying coming from inside the house. It was cold outside, but she could not feel it. She looked down to see the beautiful dress with the lace trim and blue velvet her mother had just bought her last week, along with the maryjane paten shoes to match. That day, she had had a great time with her mother, and now her mother was gone. She just did not understand why people had to die and why cancer took them so fast. Stasha felt a warm hand touch her shoulder and knew that her dad was there. Looking up, she could see the anguish in his eyes, the long hours he'd sat with Mommy, holding her hand when the pain got too much. She could feel the tears welling up in her eyes, but willed them not to fall because she wanted to be strong for Daddy. It was no use; they came down her cheeks and she could feel Daddy hugging her hard and telling her, "Don't worry, baby, we'll make it." That day, Stasha felt that nothing would ever be the same.

STASHA'S CURE

CHAPTER I

May 17, 1997

Stasha Monteau was finally going home for a much-needed vacation. Though she wished that it were for other circumstances, some things just could not be helped. Work had been so hectic for the last four months that the six-day weeks seemed like seven. By the time she got home from the office it was well past eight. Hanging her coat in the closet and walking into the kitchen, she knew that she needed to eat before getting the rest of the packing done. Mary, her housekeeper, did those little extras, which were so appreciative. As she went to the fridge and looked inside, Stasha smiled as she pulled out the fresh salad that was prepared just the way she liked it. Fresh salmon cooked and chilled, she placed the dishes on the table and turned to pour a glass of wine, thinking that it was just what she needed to take the edge off after today.

She sat down and reflected on everything that had gone on. She could not believe that Thomas Belinger could be so hard on her after all the work that she did for him. Working with the board of directors the past four months was very demanding. The research was never-ending, but to make sure that the company was going to excel in this venture was very important. To merge these two companies was going to be the best thing that she ever did. Thomas had hired her right out of university, and Stasha had worked her way up from the intern position to his right hand. It was the hardest thing that she had ever done, but if she had to do it again, would she? "Oh yes, I would do it again." Now, the company that they were merging with was going to bring Magna into the 21st century. Tantum had the best laboratories in the world and had had hard financial times in the past five years, so having these two companies together was going to help them both.

As she finished her supper, she stood up to put the dishes in the dishwasher. Turning, Stasha walked down the hallway to her bedroom. She had tried to pack all week so that tonight she wouldn't have too much to do, seemed fruitless now. Clothes were scattered all over the room and the suitcases were on the floor. Some clothes made their way into them, but most were still trying to make their way there. "Well no time like the present." It was springtime in Montreal, and the weather was always unpredictable. Stasha had her sweaters and jeans in one suitcase, and the other held her formal clothes. She knew she would be going to the club and to dinners that would be insisted by friends that needed to be attended.

Stasha took the gown out of the closet and turned to look at herself in the mirror. Holding it against her, she took a good look at herself. "Not to bad if I do say so myself." The gold shimmer brought out the gold hint in her brown eyes and gave her complexion a creamier look. Her skin was a soft bronze thanks to lying in a tanning bed once a week through the winter, and her new hair style that she had gotten during lunch yesterday made the effect she sought after just right. Her hair used to be ash brown and straight, with the length ending at her waist. Then, JoJo, her stylist, finally convinced her to do what she never thought she would do, ash brown went and put soft brown with blond highlights. The length was shortened to just below her shoulder blades, which still made it long with long layers thrown in. She loved it and wondered why it took her so long to do it. Being 5'8" was the perfect height;not too short to have to look up into others' eyes and not too tall to be looking down to people. Being slim did not come naturally, but working out four days a week at the gym made it look that way. Stasha was proud that she didn't give into all the cravings that the other people at work did. A treat occasionally was not bad. "Ok, time to get back to this or I will never catch my plane in the morning." Walking over to the suitcase carrying her casual clothes, she hoisted it up to the bed and started to arrange everything. Some more underwear and a couple of T-shirts and that should do it, Stasha thought. "I don't want to pack too much," she said, knowing that a couple of shopping trips would be worked into the agenda. After closing the suitcase and placing it by the door, she turned to the closet to get her suitcase for her formal wear.

Stasha took out the maroon pantsuit that she had worn a few times, with the tunic style jacket that formed her waist and enhanced her bust line with the straight leg pant. The soft, black, suede, open-toe pumps with the low heel went great with it, making it an outfit that could go anywhere. She placed it with the gown and a few more dresses, the black silk with the slit up the one side and the terracotta skirt with the cream blouse with tiny gold buttons. "That should about do it."

Going into the bathroom, Stasha ran a bath and added her favorite scent, vanilla musk, to the water. Undressing and pinning up her hair in a clip, she slid into the hot tub and closed her eyes, letting the water relax the muscles that she never thought she had. That week had been the hardest. The transition was on its way. When she got back from vacation, she had to meet with the CEO of Tantum. *Well let's not think unhappy thoughts tonight,* Stasha thought. Stasha had heard the rumors about Philip Demonde, but had never met the man personally. Word was that he was hardcore and did not put up with any nonsense when it came to business. As Stasha lay back in the tub, she was mentally picturing the man she would meet in about two weeks. She hoped that everything would go smoothly. It was very important for her and Magna. She was finally going to reach the goal she strived for, for so long.

The water had gotten cool, so she decided to get out and towel off. Getting into her comfortable pajamas and the old robe that had seen better days, she brought her luggage to the front door of the apartment. "At least one thing is done, now to call Dad." Stasha walked into the living room, sat down on the couch, and dialed the number she had known all her life.

The phone rang four times before being answered, "Monteau residence," came a voice so familiar that it sent shivers up her spine.

"Hello Monique, can I please speak with my father?" Stasha said, hoping that she would not give her a hard time.

"Hello Stasha, will your plane be arriving on time tomorrow?" Monique asked. "You know that we have a car that will be waiting for you at the airport and we don't want to disrupt any plans that have already been scheduled."

Stasha counted back from ten before speaking again. "As far as I know, Monique, everything is on schedule, now could you please give the phone over to my dad?" After a few seconds and hearing a muffled voice speaking to someone on the other side, he came on the line.

"How's my favorite girl?"

Stasha let out a deep breath and felt the love flow into her by those special words. Since she could remember, her dad always greeted her in the same way. "Hi Daddy. I can't wait to see you." It had been way too long. Stasha knew that she should have gone home way before now, but just could not do it. Work had been piling up with everything going on and Monique could make the strongest person want to run away screaming.

"I can't wait to see you. How did everything go today? Did you wrap everything up? I hope that I can spend a little quiet time with my girl. I planned a day so we can run away from everyone and just spend it together, just the two of us. How does that sound?"

"Oh, Daddy, that sounds great; it's just what I need right now, to spend time with my favorite guy, even if it is just a little while," Stasha said as she could feel the tears welling up in her eyes. "My plane will be on time, as far as I know, and I just wanted to find out what the weather is like there." She did not want to bring too many clothes with her.

"As far as I know from the weather network, it's supposed to be beautiful for this time of year."

"Thanks, Dad. How is everything there?" Stasha asked.

"It's ok. All the plans are working out well, but I wouldn't think otherwise with Monique at the helm. It's going to be great. The best part about it is that you will be there."

Stasha thought of all the times she could have went home and felt a little guilty. "Ok, Dad, I'll see you tomorrow. Love you."

Marcel had been waiting for weeks for this because he missed her so much. "I love you too, honey; see you tomorrow."

Stasha hung up the phone and locked everything up for the night. "Guess I'll catch a show on TV and make an early night of it." Her plane did not leave until eleven in the morning, but work had taken its toll. An early night would be a good start. Walking into the bedroom, she hung up her robe and walked over to the bed. Taking the decorative pillows off and throwing them on the chair in the corner, she pulled the covers back on the bed and climbed in. Grabbing the remote from the nightstand, she turned on the television and went through the channels, but nothing of interest was on. The news was on, and what better way to catch up on things than to watch the news. Same old stories, like which building had burned down and who had gotten injured in the car crashes, were in vivid detail. The weather said that a storm was coming in, but was forecast for tomorrow evening. Stasha hated to be in planes when a storm was brewing. Thank God her flight was in the morning. The phone rang and Stasha answered it. "Hello," she said in a very tired voice.

"Hi Stasha, how you doing girlfriend?"

Stasha smiled. "I'm ok, Franny, just tired." Francise was Stasha's best friend for as long as she could remember. Being a nurse, Franny could get work just about everywhere, so when Stasha moved to New York from Montreal, Franny moved along with her.

"Can't let my best friend go out into the big bad world all by herself now, can I?"

Franny was the best of friend anyone could ever have. They met when they first started school together and remained friends throughout all the good times and bad. Franny was very slim and petite. Her dark chestnut brown hair was short with wisp that seemed to shoot everywhere; her eyes were the darkest blue that made a person stop to do a second look. She always had a smile on her face and made a great nurse because she had compassion for everyone. Franny was there for her when Stasha's mom passed away.

"Well I'm going home tomorrow for the first time in three years. Franny, I feel so bad that I haven't gone back in so long. I know that it should have been so much sooner, but I just can't stand Monique. I swear, she just does those little things just to get under my skin." Being with her father for ten years now should have softened her feelings towards this woman, but every time Stasha tried to form a relationship with her, Monique would always do something that would set Stasha off. Stasha had been at school for about two months when her dad called and told her that he had met someone.

"I hope that you will tell your dad and Monique how sorry I am that I can't make it. With the shortage of nurses and a lot of scheduled procedures, it's impossible," Franny said.

Stasha really hoped that Franny was going to make the trip. It would have made it so much easier. "That's ok, Fran, I know that you wouldn't send me to the shewolf alone if you could help it."

"Stasha, if I can get away for a couple days, I will be on the next plane out," Franny said.

Stasha thought of all the times that she and Franny had shared. "I'll call you when I get there. See you when I get back." Stasha put the receiver back on the phone and thought about how lucky the two of them were. Not everyone could stay friends as long as they had. Franny was more than a best friend, Stasha thought of her as her sister. Stasha grew up an only child, so there were no brothers and sisters to grow up with. Franny's family made up for that. She had two brothers that were older, one with a family of his own. The oldest, Jean Paul, lived in Montreal with his wife Marie and their two little girls. Andre lived in Ottawa and was still single. Franny's mom, Evette, gave up hope that he would ever marry. Working in Parliament was a full time job. Tina, Franny's youngest sister, was a hair stylist and was hoping to open her own salon. Franny's dad, Ben, works as a carpenter and is the best in the trade. He is always being asked to do the restoration of the oldest houses in Canada. His workmanship is beautiful. He could look at a structure and copy the details to an exact match of the ones that had gone into decay. When you saw the finished product, you would swear that it was the original.

Evette had stepped in and made sure that Stasha still felt like she had a mom after Stasha's mother died. She took Stasha under her wing and treated her just as she would her own. Stasha's mom and Evette had been best friends also, so little wonder that Franny and Stasha would be the same.

Stasha turned off the television and snuggled down under the covers. "I really need to get some sleep. These next two weeks may be harder than the last four months."

The dream came back. It had been so long since it happened. It came in a rush, the air was cold, and the numbness wouldn't be shaken off. Stasha could see images coming forward, but couldn't make out who they were. The room was small and dark. There was a smell that she recognized, but just couldn't remember where she had smelled it. People were talking, but it was muffled voices. She had to get away. The feeling that harm was going to come to her was so much stronger this time. Stasha thought that if she ran again, she would never know who was there. This would always come back if she was not strong, but the feeling of wanting to run away was getting stronger. This was not the time to be brave. Stasha started to run, but didn't know where she was running to. There was no way out. Hallways turned into hallways, and around some of the corners were more walls. She started to scream, "Help me! Please, God, someone help me!" As she ran down yet another hallway, a figure stepped out and grabbed her. The arms were strong and the hands that held her bit into the flesh of her arms. As she looked up, she started to scream...

Stasha woke up in a cold sweat. Why would the dream come back now? It had been at least three years since the last one. If only she had the nerve to see the face that held her. She always screamed, and then woke up at that point. If she knew who held her, then, possibly, the dream would go away for good. Was it just that she had worked too hard the last four months that had brought it back? *Why don't I have the nerve not to run? The doctor said that I'm repressing a memory but bits and pieces would come back. However, I haven't had the dream in three years, why now?.* Stasha looked over at the clock on the nightstand beside the bed. 6:15 am. *Well, no more sleep to be had tonight, might as well get up.* Stasha got out of bed and walked into the bathroom. As she turned on the shower, she took off her pajamas, folded them, and put them on top of the shelf. Stepping into the shower, she let the hard pulsing spray take the stiffness out of her muscles. The fogginess started to retreat. Stepping out of the shower, she grabbed the towel on the warming rack. *What a great invention.* A woman at work had mentioned it and Stasha had gone out to purchase one. She hated getting out of the shower and feeling the chill. The towel came off so nice a warm. After wrapping her hair in another towel, she grabbed her robe and slipped it on. Walking into the kitchen, she started to make some coffee. While the coffee was being made, she figured she would have time to get ready. They always wanted you at the airport three hours before the flight anyway. She never thought that it made any sense. You arrived there early and waited for so long.

Walking into the bedroom, she went over to the closet and started to go through her clothes. *I want to wear something that is comfortable, but still look good. Never know when you are going to meet Mr. Right.* Stasha took the cream cashmere sweater off the hanger and thought that the taupe dress pants would go great together. They were so comfortable and looked good together. The cashmere sweater was a treat to herself a couple months ago. It sat just off the shoulders but not too much in fear that it would fall. The pants were straight waist with no pleats and had a flare on the bottom. After dressing and looking at herself in the mirror, she thought that it was just the right outfit. After doing her hair, she put on her makeup, just a little mascara, some eyeliner, and lipstick, and then she was done. Stasha was happy to be able to only have to wear small amounts of makeup because her skin was flawless, thanks to using cleansers and creams from her teenage years. "You have to work at it," Evette said, "otherwise, you will always have blemishes." And work at it, Stasha did. Going into the kitchen, Stasha poured a cup of coffee and added a little cream and no sugar. She had to watch her sugar intake; otherwise, she knew a second set of hips would start to form. Getting a bowl out of the cupboard, she poured high fiber cereal into it. Sitting down at the table, she started to reflect over the last four months.

Magna Pharmaceuticals was one of the largest companies in the United States. Getting Tantum Laboratories to merge with the company had been a work in progress for the last three years. It was up to Stasha to research the best company that could further advance Magna's work. The last four months had finally completed the deal, but much to her chagrin, she never did meet the president of Tantum. Most of the meetings had taken place with assistants and the vice president of the company. That was to be rectified after her vacation. She had an appointment to meet Mr. Demonde then.

Getting up, she went over to the sink to rinse her bowl and cup, and then put them in the dishwasher. Adding some detergent, she set it on to wash. She hated to leave it undone before going away for two weeks, it would not be wise. Going back into the bedroom, she straightened up and made the bed. Walking into the living room, she took her jacket out of the closet. Turning to inspect everything and knowing that Mary would be in to dust and water the plants, Stasha turned off the lights and grabbed her suitcases, opened the door, and walked into the hallway. Placing the suitcases in the hall, she turned and locked the door. "This is it, please God give me the strength to get through two weeks of Monique."

CHAPTER 2

It was nice when you called a car service and reserved a pick up, that they were dependable. Stasha walked out into the early morning air and smiled. "Things seem to be on the right track," she said. The car was waiting at the curb. An older man got out and came around the other side of the car and opened the back door for her. Getting in, she thought how nice it was to pamper oneself as the driver was putting her bags in the trunk. Stasha always took a cab in the city. Her car was in the parking garage. She only used it when she was going out of the city. Around the city, it did not make much sense because of the traffic and trying to park was a job in itself. Looking out the window, she looked up at her apartment building in Greenwich Village. It was a tall and beautiful building. The sandstone color gave that little hint of sparkle, which made it look so clean, and the way the windows were gave it a classic look. They were double windows with a small arch on the top. Both panes opened outward. It was nice because the screens for the windows were on the inside and didn't take away from the beauty on the outside. The apartments were very spacious, so it actually made her feel like she was in her own house. Stasha had been lucky to find this one. The couple who lived there before had been transferred for work reasons and was sad to leave. Once Stasha had seen it, she understood what they meant. It beat the little apartment that she rented five years ago. As her job position at worked climbed, Stasha kept saving her money so that she could move on to better things. Walking into the apartment, she looked no more and signed the lease right away. Stasha brought herself back to the present. They were just making their way over the Long Island Bridge to go to La Guardia Airport. The East River to Stasha was the halfway mark in her goals. She had set up goals when she was hired at Magna. She knew that she was starting as an intern and that the pay was only enough to live on in New York. The small apartment was proof enough. People were lucky to actually put furniture in it and still move around. Then, as Stasha moved up the ladder at work, using her brains and not her body, she was able to move out and lease the apartment in Greenwich. She loved it there. Not too far from work, but a better neighborhood than where she lived in before.

The next goal was to travel over Long Island Bridge to go home to a house. Somewhere near Jackson Heights. She had taken a drive up there a couple of weeks ago just to get out of the apartment. It was a beautiful day, which meant sightseeing was at its best. The houses were big and old. Stasha always liked the older houses. There was uniqueness to them, and they used hardwood that was the best. The wainscotings had beautiful designs that you could never purchase now. In her mind, she could see herself driving home from work, going down one of the tree-covered streets, and driving up the driveway to her house. The children, maybe two or three, would be in the living room watching TV. It was a dream that she was thinking of more and more lately. The first thing though was that she would have to find a man. She defiantly saw a man in the picture. She thought back about the three years with Eric, a doctor who worked at the hospital with Franny. There was a Christmas party for the staff of the hospital and Franny had begged her to go because she didn't want to go solo. Walking into La Grande ballroom astounded her. It was decorated for Christmas. All the tiny white lights made it look like stars twinkling everywhere, and in the corner was the biggest tree that Stasha had ever seen. The decorations were something out of a storybook. The ballroom itself was cream and had glitters of gold through it. Columns rose so tall, it gave a Romanesque look. It was breathtaking. That was when Stasha had met Eric. Franny was introducing her to other staff members when she turned her head and saw him. He was so tall and broad shouldered. His hair was blonde and was worn a little long. It had a shaggy kind of look to it, but not too much. He must have noticed that she was staring at him because he started to walk over.

Franny looked at what Stasha was staring at and whistled. "He is one piece of candy that I would savor for a long time."

Stasha started to laugh; Franny had a way of saying things that always brought a smile to a person's face. He was just about to reach them when she noticed that she was not the only woman looking at him. "He sure does have an effect on the opposite sex," she said. Eric was now standing in front of her and she could hear Franny in the background making the introduction, but could not register it right away. She was looking into the most beautiful eyes she had ever seen. Were they blue or slate gray? His lashes were so thick that any woman would die for them, and his face was what you would see on cowboys in the movies. He had a tanned complexion with a strong chin, and his lips were just right. Not too full, just right. The suit he was in was dark blue and fit him very well. She had to shake herself back into the present. She took his hand to shake and realized that he didn't let go, but brought her out onto the dance floor. They spent most of the night dancing away. During their three-year relationship, things had gone pretty well. In the end, Eric started to put the pressure on about marriage, but in the last year, she had noticed little things that didn't sit right with her. She started to see that he liked things done only his way. In the beginning, she just thought it was nice to have a man look after those little things. By the end of the relationship, he was telling her which dresses to wear and who she should hang around. The last straw for her was when Franny was at the apartment and had made a joke about doctors, and Eric took it seriously. After Franny left, Eric told her that it would be a good idea if she no longer hung out with Franny. He said that having a friend like her could ruin the way people look at her in the professional world. She should only be around the high crust of society. That they would open bigger doors for her, and she could only look better with having friends like them. She was so mad that she even surprised herself by not throwing the first thing in sight. She had, had enough. She had finally reached her breaking point.

She told him, "Franny is my best friend and no one will discard her from my life. She may not be rich, but she is loyal and has always been there for me."

At that point, Eric said, "Well, I really hate to do this, but I really can't have my future wife being around a woman like her. You will have to make a choice right now; it's either her or me."

She could not believe what she did next. She walked over to the closet, grabbed his coat, and then opened the front door. She told him that the choice was very easy. He grabbed his coat and looked at her. She could see the anger in his eyes.

"You do realize that if I walk out that door it is over between us."

She had never seen him so mad, but she kept her back straight and her chin up and told him that she understood. He walked out the door. As she closed it, she felt a ten-ton boulder slide right off her shoulder. At that point, she knew that she did the right thing.

Looking out the window, Stasha realized that she had arrived at the airport. She noticed it was busy for a Saturday morning as she gathered her suitcases. Walking to Gate 6, Stasha handed her ticket and passport over to the woman at the gate and checked her bags. "Now to find some coffee," she said. One cup would not sustain her for the wait that was ahead. Boarding the plane, she knew there was no turning back now. "If I could only find some even ground with Monique. She does make Dad very happy." As she sat in her seat, she thought about her father. He was always a busy man. Being in business did that, Stasha knew first hand. Monteau Industries was one of the biggest businesses in Montreal. Marcel started the company by making plastic garbage bags that could hold garbage instead of it ripping and landing on the ground. Her mom would say he got tired of picking it up off the driveway. Then, it extended into other plastic products: bubble wrap, containers, utensils, and more. Anything that could be made out of plastic, Marcel was making it. It was funny to remember how he would run to ballet recitals and class plays, never missing one.

Stasha would have understood, but he always told her that he never would have forgiven himself. When he had to go away on business, sometimes she would be able to go if there was no school. Other times, she stayed with Franny. Her dad said that education was the most important thing she would receive in life and to study hard. He never got mad if she was not doing well, but would say, "Do your best and no person can fault you for that."

A woman sat down in the seat next to Stasha and introduced herself. "Hello," she said.

Stasha returned the greeting.

"I'm Lizabeth."

"Stasha." She thought to herself that the woman was probably just a little younger than she was. "So are you going to visit or going home?" Stasha asked.

"Oh, I'm going home for a visit; I guess I just answered both your questions," Lizabeth said with a little laugh. "My family is attending an event in Montreal and wanted me to be there."

"I'm in the same predicament, but mainly I want to see my dad. Did you leave family behind?"

Lizabeth looked at Stasha and thought that she was a nice person, but kept in mind that one could never be too careful. She liked what she saw, and she didn't look like a lunatic. "Yes, I did leave my husband, Michael, and our children at home. Did you do the same?"

Stasha only wished that she could have said yes, but answered truthfully. "No, I'm not married yet and no children to leave behind, but, hopefully, one day."

Both women talked for a while, and then Stasha was getting tired. It had been a long night and she fell asleep for the rest of the trip. Waking up, she felt out of place until she realized that Lizabeth had gently woken her. Stasha laughed and apologized for falling asleep. She told her that she did not sleep well last night.

"Well at least you don't snore."

They both laughed. As the plane landed, Stasha and Lizabeth exchange e-mail addresses and told each other that they would keep in touch. Stasha was glad that she had met Lizabeth on the plane. You never knew who you were going to be placed with. She promised herself that she would keep in touch with Lizabeth. It was odd that they would get along as if they knew each other for years. They talked about their likes and dislikes and found that they both had a lot in common. Stasha liked the fact that Lizabeth didn't try to go into Stasha's past. Some things were hard to talk about.

Stasha went to the baggage claim department to collect her suitcases. Just getting off the plane and being back in Montreal brought a smile to her face. "Home," she said to herself. Looking around, Stasha realized that the PE Trudreau Airport hadn't change very much in the last three years. She saw the same hustle and bustle of commuters going to work and children running around with one or both disgruntled parents chasing them. Somewhere, she could hear a baby crying. Walking to the entrance, Stasha noticed from the corner of her eye a very tall man. She stopped to take a look. He was the type of man that any woman in her right mind would stop to admire. To take a guess, she estimated his height to be around 6'3". He had short hair in a business type style, not combed over to the side, but not combed back either. A little of both. It was a deep chestnut brown, and Stasha thought that there were probably natural red highlights, if seen in the sun. He did fill out the suit he was wearing quite well though. The jacket hung on broad shoulders then tapered into the waist. You could tell that he was in good physical shape. She couldn't see his eyes from where she was standing, but his features were not bad at all. Oh my, Stasha thought. She had just realized that while she was staring at him and admiring him, he had turned around and realized what she was doing and was looking back at her. A small and sexy smile appeared on his face, and he inclined his head slightly to tell her that he acknowledged her and turned to leave. Stasha stood stock-still and let out the breath that she hadn't realized she had been holding. "Wow, now that's what I call a homecoming, which just made my day."

At the entrance, Stasha noticed an older man holding a sign with her name on it. "*Bonjour Monsieur,* I am Stasha Monteau," she said.

"Ah, *bonjour mademoiselle,* right this way." Opening the back door of the Lincoln, he held the door for Stasha as she got in. He took her suitcases and put them into the trunk. Getting into the driver's seat, he started the car and pulled out into traffic. "The traffic is not so bad today," he said. "We are lucky that your plane arrived just after the noon rush hour."

As they went through downtown, Stasha started to recognize many of the buildings and seen a few that were new. The boutiques where she had shopped in her teens, when she finally discovered fashion, and as a young woman going off to university were still there. The restaurants where she went to dinner with her father and the theaters that he had taken her to afterwards. Her dad had instilled in her the love of the arts. They wouldn't do it often, but when they did go; her dad would make it a grand affair. He always made their time together special. Stasha remembered the first time after her mom died that he had taken her to La Grande restaurant and they approached the *maitre d'* about the reservations her father had placed. The *maitre d'* informed her father that children were not accepted in this establishment. Stasha had never seen her father mad, and by the look on his face, she could see he was very angry. Stasha remembered looking up at him and telling him that it was ok. Just as my father turned to talk to the maitre d', the owner of the restaurant came hurrying over and took Marcel's hand, "*Bonjour Monsieur* Monteau, please excuse James, he has just started with us recently." Bending down, *Monsieur* Paul said to Stasha, "How is the little princess tonight?"

Stasha replied, "Very good, *Monsieur, merci.*"

The owner stood up and told her dad that he would escort them to their table himself. As they walked away, she remembered hearing *Monsieur* Paul say to the *maitre d'* that he would return shortly to have a chat with him. Stasha felt sorry for James because he knew that he made a very large mistake. When they sat at the table, her dad asked *Monsieur* Paul to go easy on James. "We haven't been in for a while and he doesn't know who we are. A simple mistake, no?"

"Like always, a generous man *Monsieur* Monteau. If you require anything, please let me know."

That night will always stay with me because it was the first night that Dad and I went out without Mom.

As they drove away from the downtown core and to the outskirts of Montreal, Stasha realized that she felt homesick and couldn't wait to see her home and father again. "This time was way too long," she said to herself. Heading towards Ste.-Rose, Stasha knew that it wouldn't be to long now. A few more minutes passed, and they were turning on to Des Patriotes road. It looked so beautiful to her. The houses had a riverside view with lawns done to perfection. The houses in the area were large, but not mansions. The people on that street had lived there for a long time, so everyone knew each other. Her mom had told her how she had surprised her dad, and how her dad had surprised her one day. They had been married less than a year and lived in the city in a one-bedroom loft. Her dad had come home from work and her mom had a beautiful dinner waiting for him with candles and soft music in the background. Her dad looked at her mom and asked her with a smile what all the fuss was about. She said she told him how much she loved him and had a surprise. Her mom brought her dad over to the table and sat him down. After a quick kiss, she left him and went to the kitchen. When her mom came back, she was carrying two covered dishes with her and very gently placed one in front of her dad, and the other at her place at the table. Her mom sat down and told her dad that the surprise was underneath the dish cover and to be very gentle. Her dad looked confused, but loved it when her mom would play these types of games. So, very gently, he grabbed the top of the cover and removed it from the dish. On the plate were a pair of very tiny booties, and for a moment, her dad was in shock. When he finally realized what he was looking at, he looked at her mom and said, "Is this what I think it means?" Her mom nodded very slowly, and then her dad got up from the table and went to her. She stood up and her dad grabbed her around the waist and hugged her. He told her that she had just made him the luckiest man in the world. The following week, her dad went looking for houses, and when he drove past theirs, he said, "This is perfect." He had bought the house, and the following Saturday asked her mom to go for a drive with him. As they got closer to the house, her dad had told her how he needed to stop by an associate's house to have some papers signed. Her mom didn't care because sometimes that would happen. As they walked up the walkway, her mom told him what a beautiful house it was and how some day she wished that they could own a home like this one. She told Stasha that her dad's grin kept getting bigger as they got closer to the door. Her mom said that she didn't even realize that her dad had a key, but tried to stop him as he opened the door and walked in. He told her it was ok. As soon as they walked in the door to the large foyer, her mom realized that something was up. There was no furniture, but the inside was beautiful. She said that it was the house of her dreams. At that point, her dad picked her up and swung her around and said, "Welcome home, darling." Her mom said that she cried so hard that her dad thought she didn't like the house. She had to reassure him all the way home that she loved it. Her mom said that they moved in the following week.

Stasha got out of the car and thanked the driver and stood staring at the house that she grew up in. It was, in Stasha's opinion the most beautiful house on the street. It had a long driveway that circled in the front. The lawns were well manicured and the gardens that her mom put in were still there. The walkway was made of slate and placed to give the effect of a mosaic design. The house was a two-story structure of soft beige brick. The front entrance had two Roman columns on both sides and double doors. The windows in front were large and inviting. The bushes were arranged just so and were never allowed to grow beyond a certain point. Her mom wanted people to see her windows and to be able to look out of them without shrubs in the way.

As the driver closed the trunk and set her bags beside her, he wished her a good vacation and got back in his car and drove away. As the car drove down the driveway, Stasha turned to watch him go and thought, well there goes my ride. When she turned back towards the house, someone was standing in front of the doors. Stasha started walking towards him and walked into his open arms. "I've missed you so much, Daddy," she said.

CHAPTER 3

"Look who I found outside," Marcel shouted so Monique could hear him in the kitchen, leading Stasha into the foyer. "Don't worry about your bags, honey, I'll get them in a moment."

Looking around, Stasha started to notice the little changes that had taken place while she was away. The foyer had ceramic tile now in a mosaic pattern and the walls had been painted to a light taupe color. She had to admit that she liked the look.

Noticing the way she was looking around, Marcel said, "Monique and I thought that the house could use some changes, and I like the way it turned out."

In a very subtle way, her dad was trying to get the point across that it was not all Monique's idea. "I like it, too, Dad. Do I get the tour or will I have to see all the changes on my own?"

Marcel was looking at Stasha with a hopeful look, and then broke out into a smile after hearing that she liked it. He was holding his breath to see what kind of outcome was going to happen. "Let's wait until you've had a chance to rest a little, then I'll take you around. Come into the living room and I'll pour us a drink. Still drinking white wine?"

"Yes, thank you."

Marcel handed her a glass. "I better get your bags. Sit down and relax. Monique is in the kitchen and will join us in a moment."

As her dad went out to get her bags, Stasha had the chance to look at the changes in the living room. She noticed that the couch and loveseat were new. With the sandy tones in them and the high backs, they made the room look elegant and inviting. Two wing back chairs in soft gold velour sat facing the fireplace. There were little figurines on the side tables, but not so much that they looked cluttered. Looking at the big picture window, Stasha remembered all the times she would look out of it to see if her dad was home yet from work. Turning to the fireplace, Stasha noticed pictures on the mantle; still holding her wine, she walked over to look at the pictures on it. Taking a sip and enjoying the smooth taste, she noticed that some of the pictures were of Monique and her dad on various trips that they had taken. One was in Egypt and another on a cruise they had taken last year to Alaska. Moving down the mantle, Stasha realized that there were still pictures of her growing up. One was of her mom, her dad, and herself when she was five; it was the first day of school. Looking at her mom started tears to form in her eyes. Marie-Claire Monteau was a beautiful woman. In the picture, she had long blonde hair and her eyes always smile. She had the look of a woman content and happy with her life. She had just turned twenty-six in that picture. Wiping the tear that rolled onto her cheek, she was surprised that Monique hadn't taken the pictures and put them in a box somewhere in a closet.

"I know how much your mother meant to you," Monique said.

Startled by the voice, Stasha turned to face her.

"I know those pictures have a place on that mantel and that is where they will stay unless you take them down."

Stasha didn't know what to say. This woman who stood in front of her made her so mad sometimes, but hearing what she just said made Stasha think. *Maybe she wasn't the only one who changed in the last three years.*

"Stasha, I know that this is probably not the right time, since you just arrived, but I really want to talk to you. Your father and I will be married in four days time, and I really don't want to be the reason that you don't come home to see us. I have thought about the way that I have treated you in the past years and I apologize. I would like the chance to start fresh. I know that I am not your mother, nor do I ever plan to take her place in your heart. I'm just hoping that maybe we could be friends. I promise not to do things that may annoy you. I just want your father happy, and with us not getting along, it upsets him. He always walks on eggshells when you're here. If we were able to get along, it might take some of the strain off him. I would like the chance to be friends at least. I'll give you time to think about it."

Monique was turning to leave the living room when Stasha realized that not all the things that happened were Monique's fault. She had acted like a spoiled brat when they first started dating and was jealous that she wasn't the only girl in her dad's life. Maybe over the years she didn't act like the adult that she was, so Monique treated her like a child. "Monique, wait," she said. "I don't need time to think about it. I would like to try being friends also. I know that over the years I haven't been the easiest person to get along with. If you don't expect too much from me, I will do the same. I would like to be able to come more often knowing that I'm welcome and that the times here are good ones, and we won't be fighting." Monique was crying as Stasha walked over to her and hugged her tight. "We both love the same man," she said.

Monique nodded at this and hugged her back. Marcel stood in the doorway of the living room and felt like the happiest man in the world. Both of his girls had come to terms and were going to try to be friends. A man couldn't ask more than that. "So what time do I get to take my favorite women out for supper?" Marcel asked

"Dad and Monique, if you don't mind, I would like to lay down for just an hour or two. Work was tough these last four months and I didn't sleep very well last night. Are my bags in my room or in the guest room?" Monique put a smile on her face and said, "In your room. Wait till you see the changes we made." *We just had this talk and now I find out that you changed my room, the one mom and I did together.* Walking up the staircase, Stasha could feel herself losing control. Opening the door, Stasha was scared to look inside. When she did, she started to cry.

"I left everything in its original state. Marcel said I could do something with it, but this was one room that I couldn't change. Men don't know sentimental value like women do. I hope you don't mind, but I did change the carpet, but I picked the same color and freshened up the paint on the window sills."

Stasha didn't even hear her come up the stairs behind her. Walking into the room, she noticed that everything *was* the same. Looking on the far wall on the shelf were her trophies from the sports she did over the years. Everything had been dusted and cleaned. On the nightstand beside the bed her mom picked out was a picture of her mother and her that her dad had taken at the park on a sunny day. When her mom had picked out the furniture, Stasha had been seven. "We'll make the room so you can grow into it, but you will always be our little girl no matter how old you get," Marie-Claire had said. Turning around, Stasha didn't know how to thank the woman who stood in the doorway.

Monique just looked at her and smiled and said, "Take as long as you need and we will leave when you're ready. Welcome home."

Stasha walked over to the bed and sat down. She realized that she had to get over what she felt for Monique because she knew that she was really trying to get along. This was a very special gift anyone could do for someone. As she stretched out on the bed, she hadn't really realized how tired she was until she heard a faint knock on the door and realized that she had been asleep for two hours. Getting up, she walked over to the door and opened it to see her father softly walking away. "Hi Daddy," she said, trying to smooth out her hair. "I'm sorry I slept so long."

Marcel turned, "Sorry I woke you, sweetheart, but I thought that you may want to freshen up before we go out. I have reservations for us at L'Amour for eight." Stasha smiled and said thanks, then turned and started for the bathroom. *A nice hot bath should make me loosen up a bit.* She didn't realize how stressed she actually had been over the past few months. Turning on the water and adding a little scent of vanilla musk, which she loved, she took off her clothes and welcomed the heat of the water into her tired muscles as she lowered herself in. Climbing out of the tub when the water had gone cool, she combed her hair and applied her make-up. Picking out an outfit was not too hard. Growing up with her dad, she was taught how to make sure that whatever restaurant she went to, she looked good.

About an hour later, Stasha walked down the stairs. At the bottom, she could see her dad and Monique standing by the door. They really did look to be in love. Her dad was looking down into Monique's eyes and a comfortable understanding could be seen. *He really does love her, and she does make him happy.*

Monique's height was 5'4" and standing next to her dad's six feet, she seemed so small. Monique was raised in a very well off family in Quebec City. Old money, which had grown through generations of smart investors. She was a very tiny woman and kept herself in good condition. She still went to the gym every other day and even got her dad started again a few years ago. Her hair was short, which she had colored a beige blonde faithfully every four weeks to hide the gray, and it had a natural curl to it, and when styled, framed her face in soft waves. Monique's husband had died in an automobile accident about two years before her and Stasha's dad met. Monique's children, Annette and Alex, were twins and the oldest and then Mathew and Jacqueline.

Annette moved to Niagara Falls three years ago because her husband, Michael, was transferred to manage one of the largest hotels there. Their daughter Stephanie was fifteen now and going to a Catholic French high school. From what her dad had told her from the phone conversations, they loved it there. Alex, being the twin, moved close to his sister and got a job in Toronto with an ad agency and was doing quite well. His fiancé was from there. They actually met while competing for a job for a large firm. Melanie was a very independent woman, and from what her dad said, just what Alex needed. Mathew was working in Montreal alongside his uncle in the investing company Monique's family had started years ago. His wife Joan was the type of woman that could throw an elaborate dinner party, but still be able to put a pair of jeans on and big sweatshirt and be one of the girls. They had one boy, Andre, who had just turned three and another was due to arrive in the next couple of months. Jacqueline was just finishing her internship at the hospital. Being a doctor was all she talked about being. Monique was very proud of her children. Being a single parent and seeing your children grow up and being able to give them the support they needed to become what they wanted made her very proud. Both her dad and she wanted to wait until everyone was settled before thinking of themselves and Jacqueline was the last one. They thought that she would never get there considering all the schooling it took to become a doctor.

Stasha couldn't wait to see everyone. Over the years, she had gotten to know all of them and was happy that they would actually be part of the family. Being an only child with no brothers or sisters was hard and she knew that her dad tried to make up for that. In four days, Stasha would not only have two brothers and two sisters, but will be the aunt of three nieces and nephews depending on the one Joan was carrying.

"Ok you two, let's get a move on; don't want to be late, do we.

Monique and Marcel looked up startled as if they had just gotten caught doing something and started to laugh. Marcel helped Monique with her jacket and then turned to help Stasha with hers. "Can a man get so lucky as to have two beautiful women to show off?" he said as he escorted them out the door.

Arriving at the restaurant, the *maitre d'* welcomed them. "*Bonjour Monsieur* Monteau," he said. "Ah, and would these beautiful ladies be with you tonight?" Monique had a hint of a blush cover her cheeks and smiled at Marcel.

Sitting down at their table, Stasha took a moment to look around. "Dad, is this place new? I have never been here before, but I must say that it is very beautiful." The lighting in the restaurant was dimmed, just enough to make a soft glow over the gold sculptures that were placed throughout the restaurant. The burgundy drapes that hung between Roman columns gave the appearance of having your own secluded alcove. Soft music played in the background, allowing a romantic setting.

"It opened a couple of years ago," Marcel said. Reaching over to take Monique's hand, he brought up to his lips and gave it a gentle kiss.

"This is where your father proposed to me. It was so very romantic, and when he got down on one knee, I thought I would not be able to breath," Monique said.

The waiter came to the table; Marcel turned and told him, "my daughter will have a white wine, and for my lovely lady here the same. Myself, I will have bourbon on the rocks.

The waiter bowed his head slightly and replied, "Very good, sir. I will return shortly with your drinks." Looking at the menu, Stasha realized that she was not very hungry. "What do you recommend since you both have been here before?"

"The salmon is very good as is their steaks," Marcel said.

"I love the calamari, and the seafood pasta dish is heavenly," Monique added.

Stasha decided on a filet with a bourbon cream sauce with asparagus spears. After they had finished their supper, they sat and lingered over drinks. Stasha asked, "So, when is everyone arriving?"

"Annette and Michael will be arriving with Stephanie tomorrow afternoon and Alex will be here later tonight. I think his plane gets in at eleven. He said he would call. Mathew and Jacqueline said they would stop by tomorrow after Annette gets in," Monique said.

"I can't wait to see everyone, it has been a long time," Stasha added.

"The arrangements for the wedding have been all taken care of by the planner that Monique hired, so all we have to do is show up," Marcel said.

"Yes, your dad even agreed to stay at Mathew's house the night before," Monique added with a smile.

Stasha had to laugh because her dad had a look of suffering come over his face at the mention of being away from Monique for one night. As the trio got up and prepared to leave the restaurant, Stasha's eye caught a familiar face. Turning, she realized that she was looking into the eyes of the same man that had been at the airport. He was seated at a table with some other people and had noticed her as she stood up from her table.

Beautiful woman, he thought to himself.

Just before Stasha could turn to go towards the door, she saw him raise his glass to her in salute and saw a small smile appear on his face. Stasha turned and walked out the door thinking how strange it was to see the same good-looking man twice in one day, smiling to herself.

Getting back to the house, all three went into the living room and found Alex sitting in the wing chair admiring the fire he'd started in the fireplace. At the sound of Marcel, Monique, and Stasha coming into the room, he rose from the chair to greet them. Alex could only be described as handsome. Tall with sandy blonde hair that some would say was long, but kept neat at collar length. Monique was so surprised and ran over to him and gave him a big hug.

"When did you get in? It is only ten thirty and I thought that you wouldn't be in till past eleven."

Alex smiled at his mother because he always did love to surprise her. "I took an earlier flight because I wanted to surprise you; and the way you look, I guess I did."

Monique had tears forming in her eyes. Alex always had been the one to surprise her with little things. She loved it when he did. "If I would have known I would have sent a car for you," Monique said as she looked up at him.

"Mama, I know you would have, but I rented a car so that I wouldn't have to disrupt both you and Marcel. Hello, sir," he said as he shook Marcel's hand. "Stasha, look at you. How are you?" Alex said as he walked over and enveloped her in a big hug.

Stasha laughed, "Alex, you will never change. Where is Melanie? I hope you brought your better half."

Alex laughed and replied, "Am I not the better half, my soon to be little sister?"

"Oh, Alex, why must you always tease?" Melanie said as she walked into the room. Melanie kissed Monique on the cheek, and then turned to do the same to Marcel. Melanie stood just a couple inches shorter that Alex's six feet, and she was slim and carried herself well. Melanie's long red hair was twisted into a knot and small pieces seemed to fall around her face.

Walking over to Alex, she gave him a playful slap on the arm and then slipped her arm through his. "Stasha, how are you?"

Stasha liked Melanie. "I'm fine, a little overworked, but now that it is over I can rest and get back to being me."

Marcel walked over to the bar and started to pour drinks for everyone. Everyone had taken a seat and he brought the drinks over to each of them. Grabbing his glass, he made a small toast. "I would like to say to you tonight, even though not everyone is here, that your mother and I are glad that you could take the time to travel so far for this very special occasion." Raising his glass, the others joined to clink them together. "*A l'amour.*"

A couple hours passed with everyone catching up that they didn't realize that it was past midnight. Deciding on turning in for the night they all agreed to meet for breakfast in the morning. "First one to the kitchen makes breakfast," Alex said. Everyone laughed at this because they all knew that Alex would be making breakfast. He was the early riser in the family and needed his coffee before he could do anything.

In her room, Stasha changed into pajamas and climbed into bed. It was good to be home and Stasha felt that the next few days were going to be fun.

Stasha awoke with a strange feeling. Something was heavy and it was sitting right on top of her. She didn't think that Monique and her dad had gotten a dog that she was aware of. Then, she heard a small giggle and slowly opened her eyes. There was a beautiful, small boy sitting on her and a secretive smile was on his face. His sandy, brown hair was cut short and his eyes were dark blue. His little cowboy suit is adorable, Stasha thought. "May I know your name since you have me prisoner in my bed young man?

He giggled a young child's giggle that always brought a smile to an adult's face when they heard it. "I am Andre and I'm this many," he said holding up three fingers to show Stasha his age. "Are you going to get up now? Mama said that soon you will be my new Aunty."

Stasha realized that this little guy must be Mathew and Joan's little boy. "You know, someone told me that I would have a nephew soon because my papa and your grandma will be married, but I was sure that the boy would be smaller than you. Are you sure you're the one?"

Andre giggled again and said, "Yes, Aunt Stasha, it is me because there are no other little boys here, just me."

Joan came through the door that Andre left ajar and apologized to Stasha, "I'm so sorry he woke you. Mathew has been talking to him about you and he was so excited about meeting you that I guess he couldn't wait any longer."

"What time is it?" Stasha asked. Looking over at the clock on the bedside, Stasha realized that she had slept past eleven. "Oh my, I don't think that I have slept this late since I was a teenager."

Joan scooped up Andre in her arms and made a laugh come from him. "Come with me cowboy and let Aunty get up with out you getting in the way. Coffee is on and I will tell everyone that you will be down soon."

Stasha sat up in bed, rubbing her eyes, thinking that maybe she had been more tired than she thought. Taking a quick shower and throwing on a cream blouse and maroon dress pants, she walked to the mirror and started to brush her hair. A quick twist and a clip, pull a few tendrils out, and voila. She had done the same style when no time was given and worked called. Stepping into the kitchen, everyone was sitting around the table talking and lingering over breakfast. Stasha smiled when she saw Alex with an apron on. "So is there anything left?" Stasha asked Alex while taking a seat at the table. Pouring coffee into a cup and taking a sip, Stasha enjoyed the rich flavor.

"Did you have a good rest, Stasha?" Marcel asked.

Stasha looked at her father and saw the concern in his eyes. Patting his hand, Stasha reassured him that she did. Alex placed a plate of crepes in front of her and they looked heavenly. The warmed mixed berries all wrapped up in the thin crepes with whipped cream and real maple syrup tasted so good. Stasha always thought that if you were going to have crepes, they should be homemade. "Who is going to pick up Annette, Michael, and Stephanie at the airport?" Stasha asked. "I could, because I planned to go downtown to do a little shopping anyway, so would it be more convenient for everyone if I went?"

Joan looked at Mathew, and when he gave a small nod, went over to pick up Andre from his mother's lap. "Hey, partner, why don't you stay with me and Mommy can go with Aunty Stasha to get Cousin Stephanie."

Andre nodded his head and turned to his mother and said that he would stay with Papa. Joan looked towards Stasha and asked "If you're up for company, I would like to go with you, and then I could show you some of the new stores that opened since you have been here last."

Mathew groaned, knowing that he would be a little lighter in the pocket after his wife was through. Joan just smiled at him and got up to get ready.

Finishing her coffee and bringing her dishes to the sink to rinse them off, Stasha put them in the dishwasher and asked Monique if there was anything that she needed while they were out.

"No, but thank you for asking. I believe everything is taken care of."

Grabbing her coat, Stasha laughed at Joan. "I rarely get out on my own without Andre and I can't wait to have some alone time with you. You have to tell me what has been going on and why you don't visit as often." Joan was the noisy sort, but in a good way. Stasha had gotten along with Joan from the very start and felt a little guilty because she had neglected everyone for so long.

It seemed to Stasha that they had hit every store in Montreal and that Joan had an endless supply of energy. Looking at her watch, Stasha realized that if they left the mall now they would make it to the airport just in time. Her dad was nice enough to lend her the mini van, which had room for seven comfortably. At the airport, Stasha waited by the gate of arrivals with Joan. Annette and Michael emerged through the gate and were followed by this very beautiful, tall, blonde haired woman. As they came forward, Stasha could not believe her eyes. She was not a woman at all, but a teenager, and she was Annette and Michael's daughter. Annette walked up to Joan and gave her a hug and asked how she was feeling, and then Michael took his turn.

Turning, Annette shook her finger at Stasha like a mother would do and said, "I hope that you're taking care of yourself because

Mama had told us that you couldn't visit because you were working so hard."

Stasha felt bad hearing how Monique was covering for her when, all along, she knew how Stasha felt about her. What a shit I am, she thought. Stasha smiled at Annette and gave her a hug. Looking at Stephanie, she couldn't believe how beautiful this girl was. "Hi Stephanie, do you remember me?" Stephanie smiled at her mother and father, and then walked over to Stasha.

"I hear that you are officially going to be my aunt," she said with a laugh. Stasha was so relieved because, when she did visit, Stephanie would follow her around and she always had a soft spot for her. All of them went over to get their bags and, though Joan was expecting, she insisted that she could help, but no one would let her carry anything. When they got to the house, everyone was in an uproar. Standing back, Stasha felt that this must be how it feels to have such a large family.

CHAPTER 4

Everyone was awake early. The wedding planner was running around making sure that all the preparations were in place. Marcel and Alex stayed at Mathew's house. Andre was the only male in the house.

Annette was in the bedroom helping Monique with her dress and Melanie and Jacqueline were supervising the flowers and making sure they were placed where Monique had wanted them. Stasha stood on her balcony and looked over the garden. The garden in the back of the house was gorgeous. Chairs were covered in soft gold with cream ribbons tied in bows in the back. They were set in a semi circle instead of straight across, with a small isle in the middle. Monique thought it would be nice for everyone to be able to see the ceremony. It had a nice touch to it. The place where Marcel and Monique would say their vows was set with cement benches that were painted in ivory and brushed gold. Flowers were everywhere. The tent that would hold over two hundred guests was set up on the side of the yard. At the corners, it was pulled together and tied with the same gold material as the chairs and placed into soft bows. The tables were round inside the tent, ten on each side of the dance floor. The caterers had been there since early morning getting everything prepared because the reception was to follow the wedding.

Stasha thought about how many times she had pictured herself getting married here as she grew up. Stasha turned to go back into her room and finish touching up her makeup, and then headed downstairs. Her job was to keep Marcel away from Monique until the ceremony. As she was coming down the stairs, she noticed Marcel trying to be very quiet as he was walking up them. He was checking to see if anyone had spotted him and did not see Stasha standing there. As he turned his head to continue up the stairs, he saw Stasha.

"Hi honey, I was just going up to use the washroom," Marcel said with a sheepish grin on his face.

"What is the problem with the washroom downstairs, Dad?" Stasha asked, taking his arm and turning him to go back downstairs with her.

"Nothing, nothing at all," Marcel said. Knowing that he had been defeated in seeing Monique, he went with Stasha into the den.

"You know, Dad, that the ceremony will be taking place in twenty minutes, so why would you risk Monique's wrath."

Marcel walked over to his desk and leaned against it. "That was the first time in quite a while that I had not been with her through the night."

Stasha looked at her father and could see that he was upset over this. "Just think, Dad, that will be the last time you have to do that. In about a half hour, you will have every night together." As if on cue, the wedding planner walked in and told them it was time to take their places. This brought a smile to Marcel's face, and as Stasha put her arm through Marcel's, they walked out to the garden. Marcel stood waiting at the front for Monique and nodded to the many friends and acquaintances that were there to share this day with both him and Monique. They were both very happy that all their children were there also. They had thought that Stasha may not come, using work as an excuse. Marcel was very happy that Monique and Stasha had worked out their differences.

The music that started was a soft melody done on a flute. At this point, everyone stood and turned to see the bride. Alex was selected to walk his mother down the isle, as he was the oldest male of Monique's children. Monique had an ivory dress that looked wonderful on her and made her look so much younger than she was. The jacket was tapered to her waist and had very tiny pearls sewn in to make an elaborate design that swirled into the skirt. The skirt carried the design all the way down to the hem. It was a beautiful creation. As Alex joined their hands together, the ceremony started.

Watching them become man and wife, Stasha realized she was just a little jealous that her father found it twice while she was still looking. My time will come, she thought.

The reception was in full swing an hour later. Everyone seemed to be having a good time. Stasha was sitting at the table with Mathew and Joan, watching little Andre try to dance with his cousin Stephanie. The little moves he was making had more than one couple watching him. More than once, he had them laughing. Annette and Alex loved to dance and Michael and Melanie always joined them on the dance floor. Jacqueline was with some friends at another table and they looked to be having a good time. As Stasha looked around at all the people, she realized that she only knew about half of them. "See what happens when you stay away to long," she said to herself. There was a woman that she did recognize and couldn't believe she was there. Getting up from the table, she excused herself from Joan and Mathew and walked over.

Walking up to the table, she said to her "I never thought that we would meet so soon." Lizabeth looked up and gave a startled laugh.

"Stasha, how nice to see you again. Do you know the family also?"

This time, it was Stasha's turn to laugh. "Oh, yes, I know them quite well. The groom is my father."

At this, Lizabeth did laugh. Looking around the table to the people that Lizabeth shared it with, Lizabeth had introduced her to everyone. Stasha was amazed to find the one person that she thought would never be in her backyard to be sitting at this table with Lizabeth. Seeing him at a distance those two times was breathtaking, but seeing him up close was astounding. He was beautiful. That was the only thing that came to Stasha's mind. Lizabeth had said his name was Philip and that he was her older, single brother, nudging Stasha in the ribs slightly to give her a hint.

Philip just smiled at Lizabeth and said to Stasha in a warm, husky voice, "Please, you must excuse my little sister. She is forever trying to set me up with her friends."

Stasha laughed because Franny was always trying to do the same.

Looking at Stasha, Philip could not imagine in a hundred years that the woman that stayed on his mind those last few days was standing right here. In addition, to be Marcel Monteau's daughter made it all the better. Marcel was liked by everyone and Philip knew that he had a daughter who was said to be very pleasant. The only problem was that she didn't know that he was the president of Tantum. He was to meet with this woman after her vacation. Well, it would be nice to find out who Stasha Monteau was as a person out of the boardroom. At that moment, Philip decided that he would do just that. Getting up from his chair, he walked around the table and stood beside Stasha. Looking down at his sister, he said, "Poppet, I hope you do not mind if I ask your new friend to dance with me?" While saying this to Lizabeth, he had turned and was now looking down into Stasha's eyes. Not waiting for an answer, he led her out onto the dance floor. Stasha could not imagine her luck. Philip danced amazingly. He guided her over the dance floor with such grace that was hard to find in men these days. After the song was over, Philip brought her back to the table he shared with Lizabeth and his parents and asked to be excused.

Stasha was still in a dazed, but said that would be fine. She watched him walk over to her father and shake hands. Turning to Lizabeth, she said, "On the plane, you told me that you had a brother, but you left out how gorgeous he was." Lizabeth just laughed and told her that, yes, she did recall telling her that she had a brother, but to her he is just a brother who teased her growing up and admitted that maybe he looked alright. Stasha was introduced to Lizabeth and Philip's parents: Mr. Armand and Mrs. Jose LaRoch. As Stasha talked with the three, she noticed that Philip and her father were still talking. At the other side of the room, Philip had just congratulated Marcel on his nuptials.

"So you have had a chance to meet my daughter?" Marcel asked.

"Yes I did, sir, and that is why I came over to speak with you. I would like it if you did not mention my last name to her. I am scheduled to meet with Miss Monteau after her vacation," Philip told him. Philip also told him how doing business of this magnitude can sometimes bring out the worst in people. He told Marcel how he would like to know Stasha out of the boardroom and get to know her as a regular person. "Sir, please understand that I will be merging my company with your daughter's firm and would really appreciate some time to get to know her because we will be spending a lot of time working on this project and I want to make sure that I'm doing the right thing by this merge."

Marcel had never kept a secret from Stasha and didn't like the idea of doing so now. In a way, he could see an advantage come out of this. Marcel had always liked this young man and his family. They were good people, and for Philip to come and ask him to do something like this, Marcel knew that it must be very important. Plus, Marcel would not mind if Philip happened to fall for his daughter either. "Ok, I agree with your terms, but I will not have you hurting my daughter in the process."

Both men agreed, and Philip returned to his table. Marcel went over to Monique and the family to discuss what had just transpired. Not everyone liked the deception that would be played with Stasha, but if Marcel and Monique agreed, then they would also. Stasha came back from the washroom and looked at everyone sitting at the table. I can't believe this is my family sitting here. Walking over, she hugged both Marcel and Monique and decided to enjoy the rest of the evening. Philip had asked her to dance a few more times and she had the chance to talk to other people that she hadn't seen in quite sometime. It had turned out to be a beautiful day. As the guests were leaving, Stasha realized just how exhausting the day had been. She had to admit to herself that it was the first time that she had danced and laughed so much in years.

The next morning was hectic. The family was there to see Marcel and Monique off on their honeymoon, which consisted of a two-night stay at La Pural resort. Annette and Michael thought it would be a good idea to take Stephanie shopping because Annette mention to her husband that the clothes in Montreal were so different than Niagara Falls. Alex and Melanie decided to take the day sightseeing and planned to stop somewhere for lunch. Joan had a doctor's appointment and Mathew had to get back to work. Jacqueline had her next shift in a half hour that she had to get to.

As everyone left, Stasha thought how nice it was just to have the house to herself. *I am not going out of this house today. I think a nice hot bath with a good book is a great idea.* While soaking in the tub and the book forgotten, Stasha's mind drifted back to the previous day. Dancing with Philip had been very nice. They had talked very little on the dance floor, and while sitting with him and his family, she noticed they all had a great sense of humor. *Monsieur* LaRoch was very good at telling jokes. They did not touch on any business subjects, even though Marcel did tell her later that *Monsieur* LaRoch was one of the businessmen that her dad dealt with for shipping. LaRoch Shipping was one of the largest in Canada. Stasha was surprised when her dad told her because you would have never guessed it after spending time with them. They reminded her of Franny's family. Very nice people; and to look at them, you could tell that they were close.

Grabbing a pair of jeans from the suitcase and her favorite sweater, Stasha grabbed her book and went into the den. Stretching out on the couch, she started to read. There was a knock on the door and Stasha looked at the clock and noticed that she was so caught up in the book that the hours flew by. Stasha wondered who could be knocking on the door. Everyone in the family had a key, so there would be no reason to knock, and she hadn't called any of her friends yet that still lived here. Getting up and putting her book down, she walked to the front door and opened it. Stasha almost died when she realized who stood on the other side. Here she was in old jeans and a sweater, her hair in a ponytail and no makeup, and Philip stood there looking like a breath of fresh air. "Hi," was all Stasha could get out.

"Hi Stasha, I was out driving and thought I would stop by and see if you're busy. If not, would you like to go for a drive with me?"

Stasha stood there and couldn't respond right away. Stasha liked the way he filled out the Levis jeans he had on and the casual sweater in the dark burgundy and blue really brought out the green in his eyes. How come I never noticed them yesterday, she thought. Then it hit her all at once. Oh my God, she thought. I can't believe that I'm standing here looking like this. Running a hand over her hair, she thought, of all the days he could stop by, he had to pick a day when I look my worst. "I really hadn't planned on doing anything today," she said.

Philip just smiled and liked what he was seeing. Most people thought that because he was the president of Tantum that he had to have the most beautiful woman on his arm. Philip liked what was standing in front of him. The kind of woman that could put on a pair of slacks and cashmere sweater or put on a pair of jeans and sweater that seen better days, and with makeup or none she was still beautiful. He could tell that she was a down to earth person, and that made another plus towards Miss Monteau. "Well, are you busy, because, if you are, we could do it another time," Philip said.

Stasha thought that it would be a nice way to spend the afternoon. "Sure, I'd love to go for a drive, but only if you give me a minute to put some makeup on and brush my hair."

Philip had the answer he had hoped for and before Stasha could turn around he told her she looked fine, grabbed a leather coat from the hallway, and pulled Stasha out the door.

Walking to the car, Stasha gave a slow whistle. A blue and white '69 Corvette sat in the driveway. "Nice car, is it original?" Stasha asked.

Philip was stunned by the question because most women who had seen the car just thought about how much money it cost. "Actually, it was a project of mine when I was growing up. Even though I would have liked to have kept it as original as possible, some things can't be helped." Philip had bought the car from a guy when he was sixteen and worked two jobs so he could fix it up. He kept it here so he would be able to drive it when he came home. His mom kept it wrapped up for him when he wasn't here.

They drove out to the countryside. Stasha remembered coming this way with her parents to picnic. After driving for about an hour, Philip pulled into a spot that had a picturesque view of the river. He went to the trunk and pulled out a blanket and a picnic basket. Stasha started to laugh when Philip asked her where she would like to have lunch.

"*Monsieur,* what would you have done if I said no today?" Stasha said with a smile on her face.

Philip just shrugged his shoulders and started to walk to a slightly slanted hill and started to set everything up. He laid out the blanket and started to bring everything out of the basket. Stasha walked over because she could admit to herself and anyone else that the basket did smell good and she was hungry. Kneeling down on the blanket, Stasha asked if there was anything that she could do to help. Philip reassured her that there was nothing and had laid everything out. Three different cheeses, crackers, a small container of pate, grapes, sliced kiwi, and melon slices. He also had a bottle of white wine and two glasses, which he started to fill. Passing one to Stasha, he waited till she took her first sip. Stasha was amazed at the flavor the wine carried. It was fruity with a semi-sweet quality and very smooth taste.

"This is so good. Where did you buy this? I love it," Stasha said to Philip.

"You can't buy this one yet. It comes from a friend of mine who has been experimenting with different wines to see what different tastes he can get from them."

Stasha knew that she had never tasted anything like it before. After eating everything, they cleaned up and put everything back in the basket. Stretching out on the blanket, Philip motioned for Stasha to do the same on her side. Laying on the blanket and looking up into the sky, they talked for a long time, mostly of their likes and dislikes and how their days in university were. Both enjoyed talking to each other, and Philip confessed that after seeing her at the airport that he couldn't get her out of his mind. Stasha told him how she felt like a fool for getting caught staring at him, and then laughed. Philip liked her laugh because it wasn't fake. When she laughed, it came from her whole body, and it was loud. It felt good just to be with someone who was normal. Lately, the only women that he had encountered were women who expected the world on a silver platter and thought they deserved it. It was hard for him to get to know a woman who could just accept him for who he was and not what his bank account held. It was the first time that he didn't have to pretend to be anyone other than himself and to have a beautiful woman lay on a blanket beside him and talk about normal everyday things. As they lay there comfortable in each other's silence and watching the clouds go by, they both thought to themselves that it was nice.

"So when do you go back to work?" Philip asked her.

"I have another week here, and then I have to meet with the president of a company that we plan to merge with," Stasha replied.

Philip didn't know what to say. Would this be a good time to tell her that he was the one she was to meet? So much confusion was going through his mind. He was just starting to see the real person underneath the person he would meet in the boardroom. "So what is all this about, or can you tell me?" he asked.

Stasha didn't want to talk shop with him. The last four months were so strenuous and she knew that by telling him, she would have to answer a lot of questions. This was the first time that she met someone that she didn't have to be all business with. He seemed like a really nice guy. In addition, she didn't feel that it was appropriate to talk about the project with someone she just met. Today had been wonderful. "I think that it is about time that we get started back," Stasha said, then rose from the blanket and started picking up the basket. Turning, she started toward the car. Philip had hoped that by that single question that he had not spoiled what they shared today. Both were quiet as they drove back into the city.

As they pulled up outside the house, Philip asked her, "Do you have any plans for Saturday night?"

Stasha was glad that he asked because she did enjoy their time together. "Unfortunately, some girlfriends that I haven't seen in a while want to go to the clubs Saturday. Maybe if you're out, we might run into each other."

Philip planned on it. This was not the last time that he would see Miss Monteau. As Philip drove off, Stasha was thinking almost the same thing. Then she smiled. *If he is a resourceful guy he'll find me on Saturday,* as she went upstairs.

That night after supper, Annette, Melanie, and Stasha sat in the den in front of the fireplace having a glass of wine and caught up on everything that had been happening, like how Annette liked living in Niagara Falls and Melanie in Toronto. Both had seemed very pleased with their lives and their jobs. They asked Stasha how things were at work and her social life. Stasha laughed and told them that her job had finally made the breakthrough that she had been hoping and working so hard for, and social life was nil and void up until recently. Both Annette and Melanie knew who she was talking about. They had seen her face when she came in this afternoon and knew that she had a good time. Both waited till after supper to ask her, and Stasha told them she had the best time. She told them that it was nice to meet someone that wasn't in the same business she was. She confessed that he asked what she did and told them her reaction to it.

CHAPTER 5

The days seem to fly by and Stasha wished that they would just slow down. Monique and Marcel got back from their honeymoon with smiles on their faces and looked like two teenagers. Holding hands and stealing kisses. It was good to see her dad so happy again. Stasha and Monique had a truce that both hoped would last for a long time. Monique tried not to be a mother to her and, in exchange, became a good friend.

Annette, Michael, and Stephanie headed back to Niagara Falls because Michael had to get back to work. The rest had gotten on with their lives. Stasha got together with some friends a couple of nights earlier and was still recuperating from that experience. Marie and Tina, friends from school, had decided that they needed to hit the town because they had not seen each other for so long. All three had hit as many clubs as they could. She didn't see Philip that evening. Stasha found out that in the gym she wasn't hitting all the muscles in the body that she thought she had. Her legs were so sore. They tried, to Stasha's astonishment, every shot available. The trio had gotten their share of pick up lines from a number of men, also which they laughed over later. Waking up, she realized that it was so good to come back home and see everyone. She promised herself that from now on she would not stay away so long ever again.

Today was a special day. Her dad had said that this would be the day that they would be able to spend together. He would not tell her what they were doing, but promised the whole day to her. Stasha decided to get out of bed and take a shower. Stepping under the hot water felt so good on her muscles. After two days, she thought that they wouldn't be so sore. After getting out of the shower and getting dressed in some jeans and a sweater, the day was calling for cooler weather, she brushed her hair and pulled it into a ponytail. Stasha applied a little makeup so she wouldn't look so pale. She hadn't been to a tanning bed since she had been here and her tan was starting to fade. Going downstairs and into the kitchen, she caught Marcel and Monique in yet another embrace. "Ok, you two, should we just cancel today so you can be together?" Stasha asked with a grin.

"Oh, no," Marcel said after giving Monique a quick kiss. "I promised a day with my favorite girl and you will not disappoint me," Marcel said, coming over to give her a hug.

Stasha grabbed a cup out of the cupboard and poured some coffee into it. Taking a welcome sip, she closed her eyes as she enjoyed the flavor. Taking a seat at the table, she looked at both Marcel and Monique. Why didn't she see this love between them before? She had her answer in the next thought; *I was being selfish. How could I have done this to them?* Guilt seemed to wash over her. At that moment, Stasha promised to never stand in the way of their relationship and try to make things right from now on.

"Well, grab your coat and let's get on our way," Marcel said. One last kiss to Monique, he turned and started for the door. Monique told them both to have a good time and not to worry about her because she had a day set to get together with some of her friends, to discuss some of the charity events that were coming up. Stasha went over to her and gave her a hug and wished her a good day. Marcel, who was holding the door for Stasha, swelled with pride. He knew that the battle had ended between both of them and he was glad that it happened sooner than later.

Getting in the car, Stasha turned to her father and asked, "So what do you have planned for us today?"

"I thought that first we would go to that little café that we used to go to when you were younger," Marcel said. After about driving a half hour, Marcel pulled into the parking lot and they got out.

Walking inside, Stasha noticed that, even though time had gone by, some things never changed. Marcel ordered two lattes and chocolate croissants with fresh whipped cream. As they waited for their order, they sat in silence, knowing that later they would get into some deep conversation. She loved that one thing about her dad. She could always talk to him about anything.

The waitress brought over their order and as both of them dived into the creamy, chocolate treats and sip on their drinks, Stasha waited to see what Marcel had to say. She knew from the drive that something was worrying him.

"So, Dad did you and Monique enjoy your short honeymoon?"

Marcel looked at her and she could see the love that came from his eyes. "Honey, I have never been happier. Monique is not your mom, but she brings something special to our relationship. She makes me happy and I'm glad that you both are getting along."

Stasha felt guilt pull at her heart. She could have stopped the tension all those years ago had she realized how much strain it had put on her father. In a way, she was glad, too, that she put all that anger away and gave Monique a chance. Over the past week, Stasha had taken the time to know Monique and found that she was a very caring woman. Monique liked things in order and was very prompt with times and schedules. Over the years, Stasha thought that she was just being overbearing, but, in truth, she was just trying to keep things in order. Both Stasha and Monique had the chance to talk and found that they really did have a lot in common.

"Stasha, I noticed that you look tired. Are you feeling ok?" Marcel asked with concern in his voice.

"I'm ok, Dad. Just before I arrived, I had that dream again. I was so close to finding out who the person was, but then I woke up." Stasha thought as she confided in the one person she could trust. Marcel was there when she woke in the hospital. She had been unconscious for three days and Marcel had been by her side the whole time.

"Do you remember anything?" he asked. "The doctors said that you would get small pieces of your memory back," Marcel said with concern. In a way, he wanted her to remember what happened so they could catch the person responsible for putting her there. He remembered the phone call that came three years ago. No parent ever wanted to hear that their child had been beaten and left for dead. Marcel had caught the first plane to New York and had stayed with her until he brought her home two weeks later. Marcel also wanted her to forget the whole thing because he didn't want whoever did it to come back.

Stasha was a fighter though and went back to work after her bruises went away. She didn't want to let go of the project that was very close to her heart.

"I haven't had it again since I've been here, but I thought that maybe all the strain that I've been under with the project could have forced it to return."

Marcel looked worried for a minute, and then smiled. "Let's not let that kind of talk spoil our day." Marcel had hired a couple of men to make sure that no harm ever came to his daughter again. So far, they were doing their job. Weekly reports came in and they all had his cell phone number in case the need arose. "Well, if you're finished, we should head out." Marcel had been planning this since he found out that she was coming home. He held the car door open for her, and when Stasha was seated, he closed the door and went over to the driver's side and got in. Starting the car, he looked over at her and had a mischievous smile on his face.

Stasha knew that her dad had planned something special, but she could not get it out of him the whole time she had been here. She tried to get little hints, but nothing came; even when she tried to get it out of Monique, she still had no luck. Monique had told her that she was as much in the dark as she was. Marcel had only confided in Monique last night, and Monique knew that Stasha and her father were going to have a great time.

Driving into Verdun, Marcel parked close to the boardwalk and both of them got out. Marcel walked over to Stasha and grabbed her hand and said, "Now this is something that we haven't done in a long time." Marcel walked over to the bike rentals and shook hands with the owner.

"*Bonjour Monsieur* Monteau, I have your bikes ready for you. Ah, this must be the daughter you told me about; very beautiful, if you don't mind me saying," he said in a strong French accent.

Stasha smiled at him, and then looked at her dad. "So this is what you had planned," Stasha said to her dad as she got on the bike. It had been years since she had ridden a bicycle and hoped that she wouldn't make a fool of herself. They climbed on the bikes and started down the boardwalk. Stasha was having a great time now that she remembered how to ride. They biked for about five miles, looking at the sights along the river and stopping at a couple of shops along the way to look at the items people were selling. Riding back, they talked of things they remembered over the years and laughed at some of the things they had done. As far back as Stasha could remember, her father always tried to make the most of everything. Maybe it was because they both didn't have much time with her mom. After returning the bikes back at the rental shop, both Stasha and Marcel decided that it would be ideal for them to stop at a near by restaurant for lunch. They sat down in a booth and ordered club sandwiches and club soda and lemon. Looking around, Stasha could tell that this restaurant had been here for many years. It must be family owned because you could see little touches of personal effects throughout the place. Marcel was enjoying himself and was glad to have the opportunity to spend this day with his daughter.

"I see that you have been going out with Philip a lot lately. Is there anything that a father should know or do I need to have a talk with that young man?" Marcel said with a smile.

"To answer your first question, yes, Philip and I have gone on a couple of dates, and for your second question, no you do not need to talk to him. It is not that serious, Dad." Stasha liked the fact that her dad was still trying to protect her and she knew that he accepted her judgment when it came to men.

"Philip asked me what I do for a living the first time we went out and I didn't tell him. I switched the conversation to something else and he took the hint because he didn't try again," Stasha told Marcel.

"I have the feeling that I could trust him, but when I get close to someone and the subject comes up, I seem to always pull back from it. It is not a secret what I do, but this project is kept pretty hushed up and I feel that the incident revolves around it."

Marcel knew that it was the hardest part for her to work under such conditions, but it was what she wanted to do. He just wished that he never made the promise to Philip about not telling her who he really was. The one good thing Marcel did know was that Philip was a good man and he would be proud to have someone like him in the family. The one thing that Marcel promised he would never do was to interfere with that part of Stasha's life. Even though Stasha dated a couple of men that Marcel strongly disapproved of, he never put himself in the middle of it; he prayed that Stasha would see through them. In the end, she always did. "Well I can tell you that he does come from good people because I have known the family for many years. *Monsieur* and *Madame* LaRoch are very strict on family values. I guess after meeting them so long ago, that was the one thing I always remembered about them," Marcel said. Marcel paid the check and they both made their way to the car. Driving for about ten minutes, Marcel turned into the parking lot and parked the car.

Stasha looked out the window and read the sign. "Are you serious?" she said while laughing.

"This is something I've always wanted to try and I thought that I needed a special someone to share it with," Marcel added.

Stasha was so happy that he had waited to do this with her. He could have done this with Mathew or Jacqueline, but he waited for her, and that touched her heart. Walking over to the dock, the employee went over the rules and helped them on with their life jackets. Stasha could not believe that she was about to go on a jet boat over rapids with her father. Marcel was just as excited. He had wanted to try it on a number of occasions, but knew that the one person he wanted to share it with was Stasha. They started out slow and the water was calm, and then they realized that they were picking up speed. The water started to spray all over them, making their clothes wet. Then, up ahead, the rapids came into view. The excitement seemed to build up for both of them. Marcel looked at Stasha with a huge grin on his face and covered her hand with his.

"This is it, are you ready?"

Stasha laughed, she was ready for this great adventure that she knew would stay with her for a lifetime. It was a scary experience, but one that brought the thrill of it right through your whole body. Once they were on the dock, they both thanked the driver for a great time, and then headed for the car. Marcel went into the trunk and got out some blankets because they were both drenched and it was cool out. After wrapping the blankets around themselves, they got into the car.

"We will stop at home to have a quick shower and dress for the rest of day," Marcel explained.

Once home, Stasha went directly upstairs and stripped off her wet clothes. Stepping under the hot water, Stasha felt the heat go directly into her cold skin. Thinking about what they had already done today astonished her. Who would have known that her dad had wanted to try the jet boats out? Getting out of the shower and grabbing one of the big fluffy towels off the rack, Stasha dried herself off and walked over to the closet. Looking through the clothes she brought, she decided on the black dress pants and the soft, white cashmere sweater. The small pearl necklace and matching earrings that Marcel had given to her when she graduated from the university would finish the look. Stasha had known that since they were to head back out again, she wanted to look good for anything that her dad had planned. He had kept her in the dark of his plans all day, so Stasha wanted to be ready for anything. When she was done getting ready, she took one last look in the mirror and added a light rose lipstick to her lips. Walking downstairs, Stasha heard Marcel on the phone in the den. As she approached, Marcel looked up just as he was hanging up the phone.

"Anyone I know?" Stasha asked.

Marcel laughed and replied, "Well, don't you look beautiful? And, no, it was not anyone you knew." Marcel walked over to her and gave her a kiss on the cheek and could not believe how much she resembled her mother. Marcel knew that he had just married an incredible woman, but looking at Stasha, his heart tugged for a woman that he had loved fully. Time had not been long enough and, sometimes, he thought that was why he wanted to experience all the things life had to offer. Grabbing their coats, they headed out on their next adventure. Driving into the city, Stasha had the chance to look at Montreal at night. It always took her breath away. The city was so beautiful and made her proud to be a part of it.

Marcel pulled the car up to the front of a restaurant which was called *Mon Petite* and gave the keys to the valet. He walked over to Stasha and gave her his arm. They walked into the restaurant and gave their name to the *maitre d'*. "Yes, *monsieur*, I have your name right here and your table will be ready in about twenty minutes. Would you care to go into the lounge and have a drink while you wait?" Marcel looked to Stasha who had agreed that it would be alright. After seating Stasha in a chair, Marcel took the one opposite and signaled to the waiter. He ordered a scotch on the rocks with a twist of lime and ordered Chablis for Stasha. As they waited for their table, they talked about how the day had gone. Stasha laughed as she heard Marcel talk about the experience with the jet boats and laughed harder when he said he would have to get Monique on them. Stasha pictured Monique on the jet boats and smiled. Monique was willing to try anything, but somehow Stasha didn't think that getting totally soaked would be fun for Monique, but one never knew.

The *maitre d'* came over to them and informed them that their table was ready and thanked them for their patience. He proceeded to tell them on the way to their table how busy the restaurant had been since they opened.

Holding the chair out for Stasha and then seating himself, Marcel thought to himself that now was a good time as any to tell her why he brought her here. "Honey, you know that I talked to you about investing in something one day and that I held your mother's insurance money in a good money making account so that it could be invested into a project," Marcel told her, trying to make sure he said everything straightforward.

Stasha listened to what Marcel said and knew that he would never throw away the money that her mom left to both of them. Marie-Claire had also instructed Marcel to invest the money into something that would benefit the both of them. Stasha trusted her dad completely on this because he did own one of the biggest businesses in Montreal and was very smart in business matters. "Yes, Dad, and I have every faith that when that day comes you will make the right decision." Stasha knew that he was trying to tell her something and she hoped that it was not to tell her that he lost it all. There was a fair amount of money that her mom left when she died, and, by investing it, they had made a large amount more.

"Stasha, a year and a half ago I opened a restaurant because they were a good investment, if you had the right chiefs and staff. I wanted to tell you, but you were so busy. You did not visit, so I decided to wait till you came home to tell you," Marcel told her and hoped that she would not be angry with him for doing this without her knowledge.

Stasha knew that her father was having a hard time telling her this. "Dad, is there something that you need to tell me, because the way your acting is starting to scare me?"

Marcel stood up and called the manager over. "Stasha, may I introduce you to Charles, the manager of this restaurant."

Stasha looked up and told Charles how nice it was to meet him, all the while trying to figure out what her father was doing.

Charles was so pleased to meet *Mademoiselle* Monteau that he let the surprise slip. "*Mademoiselle* Monteau, it is so nice to finally meet the other owner of this fine restaurant."

After hearing what Charles had just said, Stasha turned to her father and found him smiling. "Are you trying to tell me that we own this beautiful place?"

Marcel nodded to her and asked, "You're not angry with me are you? It was a good investment at the time, and after fixing it up, it has been booked solid ever since."

Stasha was amazed. "Dad, I think that it was a great investment. Never in my life did I think that I would be a co-owner in a restaurant."

They both ordered Sirloin tip in Béarnaise sauce and grilled asparagus tips with a baked potato covered in butter, sour cream, and chives. As they ate, Marcel filled Stasha in on the last year and half. By Marcel's accounts, Stasha had a nicely growing bank account that she would have access to now that she knew, but she had asked him to keep the account for her. She explained to him that she didn't need the money, and if anything was needed in the future they would have something to fall back on.

After they finished the meal, they went back into the lounge and enjoyed some Irish coffee. After most of the questions had been answered, he had one last thing to show her. Walking down a long hallway that was only used for employees, Marcel opened a door that opened into a large area. Looking around, Stasha noticed that on one wall was a large stage with small tables clustered about, facing it. In the back was a large bar, where the bartender and waitresses were getting ready for the large crowd that would walk through the doors at nine.

"So what do we have here?" Stasha asked her father.

Marcel brought her in and introduced her to everyone. After sitting at one of the tables on the raised portion set out for V.I.P.'s, he told her how an associate of his had told him about comedy cabaret, and he and Monique had gone one night and had the best time. "I had never laughed so much in all my life, well I thought why not. We had the building and I had to find good use for it," Marcel added. "We sell tickets as a dinner package to people who want to dine in the restaurant and the others come off the street directly to the box office."

Stasha thought it was a great idea and had gone with friends to a couple in New York. She had to agree that she also had a good time those evenings. While they were talking and looking around, the place started to fill up. Customers were being escorted from the restaurant and others were being shown to their seats by hosts who stood at the door. Waitresses started taking drink orders, and for the people who did not dine at the restaurant, snack orders. As they made their way back to their seats, Marcel said hello to a few regualrs from the restaurant and introduced Stasha to them. She was not amazed that all the people she just met all had positive things to say about her father. She had to admit that it was a great idea and they had the time of their life laughing at all the comedians they had for the show that night. Stasha found out from Marcel that they only showed one show a night with as many as six comedians. He found that when he went with Monique, it was over far too quickly and he found that people liked to make an evening out of it. He opened it a year ago and, so far, the place was always filled.

On the way home, Stasha thought it would have been nice to be included in the decisions, but knew how much her father wanted everything to go smoothly before she knew. He tried to always protect her against failure, and she knew that he wanted her to see something she could be proud of. Marcel was glad that Stasha got to see the place up and running so smoothly. It was one of his best investments. Having her being proud of what he had done for the two of them made him happier about holding off telling her.

Stasha had to ask him, but didn't know how he would respond. "Dad, I have to ask you something and please don't get offended. With you and Monique married now, how does that affect our partnership with the restaurant and the comedy club?"

Marcel looked at Stasha and replied, "It's ok, honey," Marcel said, "When I asked Monique to marry me, it was her idea that papers be drawn up so that if anything were to happen with the marriage or me that she would not have any interest in the restaurant or the club." Marcel looked back at the road and told her, "Monique knew that your mother left the money to us and didn't want to interfere in something that wasn't hers."

Stasha was gaining more respect for the woman who became her step-mom just a few short days ago. Getting back to the house, they both walked into the living room and Monique was sitting on the couch doing needlepoint.

"Well, Stasha, come over and tell me about your day with your father."

Stasha sat down next to Monique and described the day to her and how Marcel wanted to have her go on the jet boats with him.

Monique laughed and told him with an astonished look on her face, "You would have me get wet my dear husband?"

Marcel went over with the drinks he had gotten for the two women and placed them on the table in front of them.

Leaning down, he whispered something into Monique's ear that brought a soft pink to her cheeks. "Ah, maybe I just might try these jet boats after all."

Stasha didn't know what Marcel said, but it must have been good if Monique was willing to get wet for it.

Monique turned to Stasha and asked her what she thought of the restaurant and the club.

"I was so surprised," she said. "Here I thought that Dad was taking me to this beautiful restaurant, and then to find out that I own half of it. I was truly amazed." After telling Monique about their day and finishing her drink, she said good night to both of them. It had been a long day and, while climbing the stairs, Stasha had reflected on all of it. Closing the door to her bedroom, she took off her clothes and put them away. Putting on her pajamas and climbing into bed, Stasha lay there reflecting on everything that had changed since she was back home. As her eyes started to close, she realized that the only thing she lacked now was a man in her life and hopefully a family one day. On that last thought, she went to sleep, not knowing that someone else had the same thoughts on his mind, but for the deception he put into play, he thought he just might lose something that he just found.

CHAPTER 6

It seemed like the two weeks flew by, but Stasha knew that work was waiting for her and the meeting with Mr. Demonde was scheduled for tomorrow. She had everything prepared, but wanted to go over everything just to make sure that she didn't miss anything. Gathering up her luggage, she brought it downstairs so the driver could bring it out to the car. Marcel and Monique stood by the door waiting for her. Stasha told her father that she would not stay away so long next time and gave him a big hug and kiss on the cheek. Turning to Monique, she said," I am so glad that we had the chance to fix everything. I'm so happy for you both."

As she said that, tears welled up in Monique's eyes. She felt the same way. Monique had hoped for along time that she and Stasha would become friends one day since they both loved a very special man.

As Stasha got into the car, she waved one last time at them and closed the door.

Stasha didn't have time to reflect on everything that had transpired over the last two weeks. She had turned into business mode and knew that the meeting coming up was the most important one yet. Not only would it bring Magna financial gain, her project, if done properly would be life saving to millions of people. Looking back, she realized that she had been working on this project for years and one man could destroy everything in a single moment. Stasha got out of the car at the airport and went to check in at her gate. As she stood there, she looked around the airport at all the people traveling to so many different places. Out of the corner of her eye, she recognized someone. Philip stood there looking at her with a huge grin on his face and started to walk over. Philip had taken her out a few more times while she stayed at her father's house and they had gotten along quite well. As Philip drew near, Stasha asked, "Where are you headed to?"

"I'm going to New York. Since I'm headed your way, I thought you might like a lift?" Philip asked with a grin.

Stasha laughed and accepted. "The company I work for lent me the company jet so I could come home for a little R&R, so, since I knew that you were taking a flight home today, I thought that I would leave as well and see if I could catch you before you left."

As Stasha's luggage was being transferred to the other plane, Philip fixed drinks for both of them. "We have a few minutes before we can take off, so I thought maybe we could have a drink," he said as he passed her a white wine.

"Nice plane, you must be your boss' favorite for him to lend you this for a vacation."

Philip thought in the back of his mind that now would be a good time to tell her, but he just couldn't do it. The dates with Stasha were incredible. She was like no other woman that he had dated. When she laughed, it came from the soul, and when she smiled at him, it was like no one else was in the same room. The main thing was that, even though he was one of the richest men in the world, in her eyes he was just Philip LaRoch. Ok, he thought, she doesn't know that I own Tantum yet, but if she could continue to just like me for who I am, then maybe it won't be as big as a hurdle as I think.

Philip remembered the day of the wedding; he had seen this beautiful woman in a soft gold dress that seemed to hug every curve. When she turned around, he felt like someone had punched him in the gut. Then he found out that she was *Mademoiselle* Monteau. During the plane ride home, they talked about everything except business, which was fine with him. He knew that the time would come to tell her the truth, but not now. Right now they were finding out things about each other and seemed to have a lot in common. Stasha told him about the restaurant and the comedy club, and he had told her, he and some friends had made an evening there with supper and show and the great time they had. He thought that it was great that someone could go for the evening instead of a few hours to catch the show.

Philip also told her how thoughtful it was for her father to surprise her like that.

The landing was very smooth. While waiting for their bags to be loaded into the cars that were waiting for them, Stasha gave him her number and Philip agreed to call her within the next few days. As Stasha got into the car, Philip leaned down and gave her a soft kiss on the cheek. Closing the door, he waved to her as the car drove her home.

Stasha was glad to see her street as they turned the corner and her apartment building was in sight. As the car pulled up in front of the building, Stasha was glad to get home. Getting her keys out, Stasha put the key in the lock and opened the door. The apartment smelled fresh. After putting her coat in the closet and throwing her keys in the bowl she kept on the table in the entry, Stasha looked around. Mary had come in to water the plants and brought in the mail, which Stasha looked through quickly and would go through later. Mary had the place nice and clean and had put some fresh flowers on the dining table. Grabbing her luggage, Stasha walked towards her bedroom and started to put everything away. She hated to leave it because she would eventually have to do it anyway. After getting everything sorted and put away, Stasha walked into the kitchen to fix something to eat. Going into the fridge, she gathered some brie cheese, grapes, and some crackers and arranged them on the platter she used for this type of snack. She thought that she would have to pick something up for Mary because she always made sure that Stasha had groceries and everything was always fresh. Putting the platter on the table and pouring herself a glass of wine, Stasha walked over to the fireplace and turned it on to a small flame. Having the gas fireplace added a nice touch to the living room. Sitting on the couch and curling her feet under her, Stasha reflected on everything that had happened over the last two weeks. She was happy that her father was happy. It was also nice to know that she and Monique had taken the time to rectify the differences they had between them. She had the chance to be at the special event and, in the process, met a very good looking man who was also a very caring, family orientated person. It was nice to know that there were still people who cared about their family members. Being out with her friends also brought back memories of the university days.

The phone began to ring and brought her back to reality. Putting down her wine, Stasha reached over to pick it up. "Hello," she said into the receiver.

"You're home. That's great. I hope you're up for a visit because I'm on my way over," Franny said.

"Hi Franny, sure come on by. I'm going to hop into the shower, so I should be done by the time you get here. See you soon." Since Franny was coming over and it was almost time for supper, Stasha decided to put something in the oven. Going to the freezer, she took out a couple of marinated steaks and put some baked potatoes into the oven. Stasha would get the vegetables done after her shower. Walking down the hallway to the washroom, Stasha turned on the shower and took off her clothes. Stepping under the strong spray of the hot water, it felt good to wash away the travel weariness that had worked into her body. Stepping out and grabbing a towel off the heating rack and drying herself off, she headed off towards her bedroom to dress. Stasha decided to put on a velour pant set because she could dress for relaxation around Franny. Combing her hair and looking into the mirror, she knew that she could leave her face free of makeup because Franny didn't care what she looked like. Their friendship was rock solid. Just as Stasha was walking towards the kitchen to check on the potatoes, the door bell chimed. Opening the door, Stasha had to smile because here was Franny with a big smile on her face and holding a bottle of wine in her arms.

Franny walked into the kitchen and put the wine in the fridge, then gave Stasha a hug. "So how did it go?" Franny asked while turning back to the fridge to get some vegetables out and start preparing them.

Stasha turned on the grill and grabbed some dishes out of the cupboard to start setting the table while it got hot enough to grill the steaks. After that chore was done, Stasha turned to see Franny holding a glass of wine out for her. "Thanks," she said while putting the steaks on to cook. Stasha loved her stove. One could do just about everything with it. It cost more than what she wanted to spend, but with the grill and double oven she couldn't resist.

"So are you going to tell me what transpired while you were gone or am I going to have to pull it out of you?" Franny asked.

Stasha smiled and told her that she would just have to wait until they sat down to eat. Once everything was placed on the table, Stasha told Franny how Monique had changed the house and the surprise with her room. She also told her about the long talk they both had and how they decided that it was foolish to always be angry with each other. Stasha told her about the wedding and how well everything went.

After finishing supper, both girls cleaned up and put everything away. Pouring another glass of wine, they went into the living room to relax on the couch. Both took an end and had their feet up so they touched in the middle. They had sat that way since they were children, and it came naturally to do the same even though they were older now. Stasha told Franny about the restaurant and the comedy club that her dad had bought and opened for them.

Franny was amazed that so many things happened while Stasha was away and disappointed that she wasn't there to share it with her. Franny asked about everyone and was happy that no one was sick and that they all made it to the wedding. Franny told Stasha how they were so short of nurses at the hospital that she ended up working a few double shifts. Franny didn't mind because the extra shifts put money in her savings account and she hoped to move out of the city and buy a home in the near future. As they sat there in front of the fire and sipped their wine, the door bell rang. Stasha looked at Franny and told her that she wasn't expecting anyone. Franny got up and went to the door with Stasha. Stasha looked through the peep hole and saw a delivery person standing there. Opening the door, he asked if she was Stasha Monteau. She said she was and he had her sign for the delivery. As he stood back, two men carried in two large bouquets of the most beautiful flowers she had ever seen. After closing the door, Stasha turned towards the flowers and took the card out of the first bouquet.

Leaning down to smell the flowers, she straightened up and read the card. It read: *Hope you made it home safely and can't wait to see you. P.*

Franny, who was standing behind Stasha as she read the card, walked over to the table and picked up her wine. After taking a sip, she waited for Stasha to say something. "Ok, what really happened to warrant all these flowers being delivered? And who is 'P'?" Franny had to get the scoop because she had never seen such beautiful bouquets delivered to anyone. As she waited, Stasha was trying to figure out how to tell Franny without making it into something more than what it was. Walking over to couch, Stasha grabbed her wine and motioned for Franny to take a seat. Franny walked over and could see that Stasha was going to try to hold something back, but, being friends for so long, Franny had the knack of getting things out of her.

Stasha had told her how she had met Lizabeth on the plane and how they talked about different things and how Lizabeth was going home for an event. She told Franny how she had saw this gorgeous man at the airport and got caught looking at him. Then about seeing him again at the restaurant that evening when she went for supper with Monique and her dad. She continued with things being very hectic at the wedding ceremony and her not noticing Lizabeth until the reception. While talking to her and being introduced to her family, which had turned out to be good friends and business associates of her father, Lizabeth had introduced her to her brother, who happened to be the man she saw at the airport and the restaurant. They had danced, and over the two weeks had gone out a few times.

Franny was amazed and happy for her. It had been a few years since Eric, and Franny knew that she went out on dates, but she had not seen *that* look on her face like she just witnessed, when the flowers arrived. Franny realized that her friend might have found someone who she could relate to, and he seemed like a thoughtful man from what Stasha said.

They laughed over the tale of Marcel and their wild trip on the jets boats and laughed harder when she told Franny about the look on Monique's face when Marcel suggested that she try it with him.

It was getting late, so Franny got up and went to get her coat.

"I'm glad you're back. I'll call you tomorrow after work to find out how your meeting went with Mr. Demonde. Hope everything goes well."

Franny left and Stasha decided that the best thing to do was to go to bed. Like Franny reminded her, the big meeting was scheduled for tomorrow. Stasha had the good sense to make sure that all the papers were in order at work before she left for Montreal. Her presentation board was also in her office. Checking that everything was locked up for the night, Stasha turned off the lights and headed for the bedroom. Reaching her room, she undressed and put her pajamas on. Climbing into bed, Stasha laid there, satisfied that tomorrow would go well. The president of Tantum would be nuts not to merge with them. All the traveling that she had gone through had finally caught up with her because she was asleep a few minutes later.

The alarm was going off and Stasha stirred from sleep and realized that today was the big day. For all the work she went through, she was finally going to make a presentation to the one person who could make the difference in the project that had consumed her thoughts for years. Magna would also be able to use the resources that Tantum had to bring other projects forward. In return, Tantum would have the use of all the contacts that Magna had on file to bring a wider business base to Tantum Laboratories. Stasha went over to her closet and picked out a black pant suit and chose a dark blue chemise to wear underneath the jacket. Sweeping her hair up in a French knot and applying her make-up, she checked in the mirror to make sure that everything looked ok. Satisfied with the look, Stasha went to the kitchen to put on coffee and poured herself a bowl of cereal. She learned a long time ago not to go into a meeting on an empty stomach. After having breakfast and putting everything away, Stasha went to the closet and grabbed her coat. Picking up her briefcase and her keys, Stasha headed to work.

Arriving at work, Stasha greeted people as she walked by. She knew that if she treated people well that they worked that much harder for her. She never passed someone without greeting them. That was probably why the staff she had never had a bad thing to say about her.

Walking into her office, she went through her messages and sorted them out from the urgent to the ones that she could hold off until after the meeting. The meeting was scheduled for one o'clock, so that left Stasha with time to catch up on some work that had been left since she went away.

Tara, Stasha's secretary for the last six years, came into the office with two coffees, one for Stasha and one for herself. Putting Stasha's on her desk, Tara took a seat in the chair in front of the desk. "So did you have a good time and how is the family?" Tara asked.

"Everyone is fine. I had a great time," Stasha replied.

Tara had moved up with her with every promotion that Stasha received. It was part of her contract and Stasha liked the idea of it, because training a new secretary would be a hassle. Tara knew how Stasha worked and how the job needed to be done, so it saved Stasha time and Tara was a godsend. She started out of college at the age of twenty-two, and proved to Stasha that she was the one for the job.

After six years, Stasha had never had any regret about hiring her. Tara had just starting seeing someone, but Stasha had not met him yet. She knew that if Tara ever married and had children, she wouldn't have to worry. Four years ago Stasha and Tom Belinger put a daycare centre on the bottom floor of the building so that employees could have their children close to them. The employee daycare prices were cheaper, which kept workers happy, making good workers for the company.

Stasha went through some letters that needed to go out and dictated some more that Tara would have ready for her to go over and sign before she left for the day. By the time they finished and Stasha had called back her urgent messages it was eleven thirty. Stasha went to have some lunch before the meeting. Walking by Tom's office, she poked her head in to say hello. Tom was just getting off the phone and got up to put on his jacket.

"Are you ready, Stasha?" he asked as he walked over to the mirror on the back of his door to make sure that his jacket wasn't wrinkled.

"Yes, I have everything in place. I can't see how he could walk away from one of the best offers that he is ever going to get," she said, confident that things were going to go smoothly.

Tom was taking Mr. Demonde to lunch, and then both of them would come back to the board room where Stasha would be presenting. Stasha and Tom thought that it would be a good idea to have her set up so that when Tom got back, the meeting could start right away. Plus, it would give Tom a little extra time at lunch to get a feel for Mr. Demonde.

Stasha went down to the cafeteria and had a salad and a green tea. She didn't want to have anything to heavy. After finishing, she decided to go and get the boardroom ready for the meeting. Tara had met her there and they went to work. By the time everything was in place it was five minutes till one. Tara just finished filling the pitcher with fresh water, and then took her seat. She was going to take notes of the meeting for Stasha to look over later. Stasha was seated in her chair looking over her notes when Tom and Mr. Demonde walked in. She looked up and smiled at both men. When she realized who Mr. Demonde was, the smile died on her face. Philip knew at that moment that he had waited too long to tell her. Stasha could not believe that the man she had known for two weeks was not the man she knew at all. The meeting went as scheduled and Stasha answered all the questions that Philip had asked. Through the meeting, Stasha went from feeling like a fool to becoming very angry, but was not about to let him know how much it really affected her. At the end of the meeting, Philip had told Tom that he was satisfied with the presentation and was looking forward to working together with Magna. Philip asked Tom if he could have a few moments alone with Stasha so they could talk about the projects that they would be working on together.

Tara had known that something was wrong the moment both men walked into the room. Tara got up and walked over to Stasha. "Do you need me to stay to take notes?" she asked her, and saw the anger in her eyes.

"No thank you, Tara. I think that Mr. Demonde and I need to discuss some things in private. I will go over those notes with you later."

Tara left on that cue and knew that Stasha would not be a happy camper when she got back to the office. As Tara and Tom left the boardroom, Stasha started to count to ten.

Looking up and into Philip's eyes, she asked him "So when were you going to tell me who you really were?"

Philip knew that she was angry and knew that he went about everything all wrong, but he also knew that he had fallen in love with her in their short time together and was not about to let her go. "I know that I should have been honest with you, but I wanted to find out who the real Stasha was since we would be working together on a lot of different projects."

Stasha got out of her chair and walked over to the window. Looking out, she wondered if anyone could be so low as to not tell someone who they really were. Turning, Stasha said, "I can't believe that you would use me as if I was a tool in your lab. I really enjoyed the time we spent together, and the flowers that you sent were beautiful, but it was just a game to you, wasn't it?"

Philip wished that he could go back in time and change it all. Stasha turned back to the window wondering how many people knew just who he was when she went home. Philip came up from behind her and took hold of her arm to turn her around. Mistake number one, because when he turned her to face him, Stasha brought her hand up and slapped him across the face. Tears were in her eyes. As she started out the door, she turned to him and told him, "You know Philip; I had the best time in Montreal. The one thing that I never would have imagined was that you would be such a bastard to do something like this to someone. I want to ask you one other thing. Did my father know that you were keeping your identity from me?"

Philip was still standing by the window. When he looked up, he didn't have to answer her question because she saw it in his eyes. Tears then began to fall. As Philip went to go to her, she held up her hand and shook her head because, at that point, words would not come. Stasha felt that the day was one of her best because the goal she wanted was achieved. On the other hand, it was one of her worst because her father kept this secret from her; and the one person she started to care about played such a vicious game. At that point, she opened the door and walked blindly towards her office as the tears fell down her cheeks. Stasha couldn't believe what had just happened. As she walked into her office, she turned and closed the door. Tara came in and went over to her. Holding out her arms, Stasha walked into them. Tara knew something was up, but she would let Stasha tell her in her own time. Tara had worked for Stasha for years and was there to hear Stasha vent about Eric, and no doubt there would be more venting by the way things went today.

After calming down and grabbing the tissue that Tara held out for her, she wiped the tears away and went to sit in her chair. "I can't believe that he would do that. Why didn't he just tell me who he was?" she said to Tara. The only thing was, that she didn't tell her about Philip yet, so Tara was just going to listen until it all came out. "Tara, I think I'm going to go home. Could you please rearrange my appointments till tomorrow?" she asked.

Tara knew that she was having a hard time and was trying to keep it together until she left the office. "No problem, why don't you go now while everyone is busy."

Stasha got up and grabbed her coat. Walking past Tara, she told her thanks and she would call her later. As Stasha got on the elevator, Philip walked out of the boardroom and was determined to talk to her before it went any further. She was right to call him a bastard, because if she didn't, he would have called himself one. The look on her face when she realized who he was when he walked in that room was like a kick in the gut.

Philip asked a person walking by where he could find Stasha's office. After getting directions, he proceeded down the hall. Once he arrived, Philip asked Tara to tell Miss. Monteau that he wished to speak to her.

Tara looked up and really couldn't believe that he would have the nerve to come to the office after what he did. He was the reason why Stasha was crying when she came back to her office. "I'm sorry, but Miss Monteau has left for the day and will not be returning until tomorrow. Would you like to leave a message for her?" Tara had a little sting in her voice, but she reasoned that she was a little protective of her boss and friend. Philip knew he had some work to do now.

CHAPTER 7

Stasha was numb all the way home. Questions for her father were going through her head, but she knew that she would wait to calm down before calling him. Walking into her apartment, she shut the door and leaned against it for just a moment. Closing her eyes, she took a deep breath. Opening them, she put her coat over the sofa and went to pour herself a glass of wine. Looking at the clock, she knew that she could reach him at the office. She picked up the phone and dialed.

"*Monsieur* Monteau's office, how may I help you?" his secretary asked.

"*Bonjour* Edna, this is Stasha. Would my dad be available?" Stasha tried to keep her voice steady. Edna had known Stasha since she was a little girl and she didn't want to answer any questions Edna may ask.

"Oh, hello Stasha. Yes, your father is always available for you. Just hold one minute and I will transfer you through." Stasha waited to hear the voice that had comforted her through so many times growing up.

"Hello, honey, is everything alright. I thought that you would still be at work. Did the meeting go alright?"

There was a question in his voice and Stasha finally realized that he knew about Philip's true identity. "Why, Dad, why didn't you tell me?"

Marcel heard the hurt in her voice and wished that he had never promised Philip to keep quiet. "Honey, he wanted to get to know you for who you were. He has worked with a lot of people who always played up to him because he was the owner. He knew that he would be working with you personally on this project and wanted to know the real person," Marcel wanted her to understand that he would not have done something like this to her.

Stasha knew that her father would never intentionally hurt her, but she needed to hear it from him.

"Stasha, you went out with him so many times, did you not even ask the man his last name?"

Stasha just presumed that his last name was LaRoch.

"Stasha, you know that I would never hurt you. This man that you got to know is a good man and comes from a strong family. Let me ask you a question, how would you have treated the man if you would have known that he was the owner of Tantum? Would you have had a good time getting to know him or would you have tried to impress him, knowing you would have a meeting with him when you got back?"

Stasha knew that her dad had just hit it on the button. No, she wouldn't have gotten to know him for who he was, and, yes; she would have been trying to impress him the whole time. "Ok, Dad, you know me too well. It was just a shock to see him come in and having to keep it together in front of Tom and not let it show."

"Well how did the meeting go?" Marcel knew that it was very important to Stasha that she have access to the labs.

"It went better than I thought, but being so upset I really don't know if he signed the papers or not. Plus, I called him a bastard before I left."

Marcel winced on the other end of the phone. "Honey, give him a chance to explain. If you still feel the same, then I will stand behind you."

Stasha knew that he would. "Thanks, Dad. I'm sorry that I jumped the gun. I'll think about what you said. Love you." Stasha hung up the phone and sat on the couch thinking about what her father told her. He was right; she just presumed that his name was LaRoch and not Demonde. She was also the one who didn't want to talk about work when he had asked what she did for a living. She also would not have had as good a time with him if she would have known who he was.

Sitting there and sipping her wine, she realized that he wasn't the only one at fault. She could have asked personal questions too. She winced when she realized how she called him a bastard and the look on his face when she walked out. "Oh my god, what have I done?" Stasha exclaimed. Putting her coat on, she rushed over to the door. She had to get back to the office and hope that he was still there so she could apologize. How could she jump the gun so fast? Here she thought she was a level headed person, but, in truth, she felt like the biggest fool. Pulling the door open, she almost ran right into him. Philip stood there poised to knock when Stasha pulled the door open.

"I want to talk to you, but I see that you're on your way out. Can you call whoever you were going to see and reschedule because we need to discuss some things?"

Stasha stood there in shock. Here she was just running out to find him and here he was standing in her doorway telling her they needed to talk. Stasha almost laughed to herself. She stood to the side and allowed Philip to come in. Philip couldn't believe his luck. He told Tom what happen so Tom would give Philip Stasha's address, so he could come and explain himself. He left Tom laughing because Tom figured something must have happened between the both of them from the looks they were passing between them through the whole meeting. Philip looked around the apartment while Stasha put her coat away and went to fill her glass of wine.

"Would you like something to drink?" she asked him. Philip agreed to a beer and went to sit on the couch.

He liked her style. The place had crisp cream walls with the rest of the colors coming from the drapes, furniture, and pillows. It felt nice, a place where someone could entertain with ease. Stasha handed his beer to him and sat on the couch beside him. Turning towards each other, Philip started to tell her how sorry he was, but Stasha raised her hand to stop him. "You know that you're the only woman that I have allowed to raise her hand to me and still talk to?" Philip said with a grin.

Stasha was determined to be the first to speak. "First of all, I want to say I'm sorry for slapping you. Second, I was wrong to act the way I did." Stasha knew it was important to her to make sure that he knew that she just didn't go around slapping men. Philip had to explain to her why he did what he did and to rectify the situation.

Philip looked into her eyes. Those eyes haunted his dreams and he knew that he was starting to have feelings for this woman but wanted to get past this first. "Stasha, I have to tell you why I didn't tell you exactly who I was. You have to understand that when I meet someone, I never know if they are truly there for me or my money. I wanted someone to like me for myself, and I knew that we would be working together for a long time. People think that I take things for granted, but you met my mother, she would never allow that."

At this point, Stasha laughed out loud. She found out herself how Philip's mother expected her children to act. She loved every one of them, but she would never let them forget their roots. Philip took a drink of his beer and hoped she understood what he was trying to say. The last two weeks had been great and he didn't want to screw it up, even though he knew he came close to doing so.

He waited to see what she would say. Stasha sat there for a minute just looking at him. She knew what he was trying to say because she had been in the same position a time or two. As soon as they found out who her father was, they changed right in front of her eyes. Everyone wanted to be her best friend.

Stasha looked at Philip and said, "I understand why you did this. When you caught me going out the door, I was on my way to find you to apologize. When I found out my father knew, I called him and he made me realize that I was as much at fault as you were. I never asked your last name; and when you wanted to talk about work, I was the one who stopped you." Raising her hand, she gently put it to his cheek and looked him in the eyes. "Can you forgive me, Philip?"

Philip had his heart in his throat as she talked; now all he wanted to do was kiss her. Stasha had tears forming in her eyes as Philip put his beer down and ever so slowly leaned over and touched his lips to hers. The kiss was nothing that Stasha had ever felt in her life. His lips felt like heaven and she couldn't help herself from deepening it. She opened her mouth just enough to give him the invitation. Philip didn't think, but took what was offered. Holding her in his arms felt so good. He had dreamed that this was what it would feel like. Slowly, the kiss ended and they remained holding each other. Stasha didn't know what to say, so she just stayed in his arms. Philip knew that after spending time with her, that she would be the type of person who gave and didn't take. He felt great; it was the first time that he kissed a woman that didn't expect anything from him. There was nothing false about it.

As they sat there, Philip told her that he wanted to take it slow; Stasha agreed. Getting up, she got him another beer and poured herself another glass of wine. Stasha realized that it was almost five and asked Philip if he would like something to eat. Philip had never turned down food in his life. Even though his body was solid, he always gave in to the indulgence of food and worked out that much harder at the gym the next day. They both went into the kitchen. While Philip put a salad together, Stasha put some lasagna in the microwave. Mary always made sure that Stasha had some easy meals to prepare fast because when she was into her work she did not take the time to fix herself something. Stasha also took some rolls out and put them in the oven to warm while Philip set the table.

As they ate, Philip told her some of the projects that he was working on and how he looked forward to starting hers. After supper, when everything was cleaned up, they decided to go sit back in the living room. Stasha turned the fireplace on to a small flame and sat down on the couch. Sitting next to Philip as he put his arm around her, they talked about his family. Stasha learned that Armand LaRoch was his stepfather, and how his really father died when he was two. Armand had treated him like a son ever since.

"Why didn't he adopt you since you were so small?" Stasha asked out of curiosity.

Philip told her how his grandfather owned Tantum before him, and his father who worked by his side was the next to inherit. After his dad died, his grandfather knew that his mom would eventually remarry; he never expected her not to. His grandfather stipulated in his will that Tantum would go to him when he experienced enough to take over as long as his name stayed Demonde. "You see, Stasha, my dad was an only child; if Armand adopted me, then my name would have changed. I am the last in the line in my family to carry this name, and it was important to him and me that it stayed alive." He told her how it was growing up with his sister, and how hard he worked with his grandfather to achieve the right experience to take over the company. "Grandfather was a hard task master and trained me himself. Tantum is growing all the time, but by merging with your company, I have just given it a bigger base to work from," Philip explained.

Stasha didn't know what to say. She knew how it was growing up without her mom. Losing a parent was the hardest thing she ever had to face. Philip was two when his dad died, Stasha had been seven. She remembered her mother and still missed her. She told Philip about her mother, how beautiful she was, and the special times that they had shared. She also told him about the cancer that came so fast and took her at the same speed. "One day, Mom and Dad told me she had cancer, and after a couple of months she was gone." She told him that when she was young and kids told her how either a parent or someone they knew had cancer, Stasha presumed that that person would die quickly, too. Some people did, but a lot of them didn't and survived. She felted robbed when they would survive because her mom didn't. Her dad tried to explain to her that it happened that way and her mom's cancer was too far gone for them to do anything about it. Philip knew why Stasha had started the project now. Stasha explained to him why it was so important that people have something to tell them when their white blood cell count was high, so they could be looked at by a professional doctor.

Philip thought it was a great idea and that was why he would be working on this project with her. He wanted to make sure that it became successful. Not only would it put Magna and Tantum on top of the business world, it would be able to give people with any life threatening illness a chance to get to a doctor and have it diagnosed before it became life threatening. The imbalance in the blood would be detected by this small hand held computer that took the sample, and then ran it through a screen test. At this point, it would inform the doctor which area needed more tests. It could save millions of lives. Philip now knew the reason why Stasha worked so hard to get this accomplished. If her mother would have had a device like this, she may have been able to get to a doctor sooner.

Stasha also told Philip about the night that she was working late on some research for the project and she was the only one in the building because everyone had gone home. She wanted to get this one part of the research done. She was working on this after hours. There was other work to do at Magna that took a lot of her time, so she stayed late to do research and build her dream into reality. She had just left her office around ten o'clock and was walking down the hallway towards the elevator. Then, she woke up in the hospital and her father was sitting beside her. Apparently, someone had been in the building and Stasha got in their way. At least that is what she thought because she couldn't remember what really happened. Philip was about to ask her if she was afraid to work in the building now, but Stasha beat him to it. She explained that Tom no longer allowed her to stay past five. In the winter when it was dark outside, one of the security guards would walk her to the front and another would make sure that there was a cab waiting for her. Tom knew how important this project was and wanted to make sure that the person who was responsible for bringing it to life kept her own also.

Philip sat there while she explained everything, and got a little worried when she came to the point of being attacked in her own building. He was glad that measures were in place to make sure that nothing happened to her after that, but he made a mental note to look into it himself. Stasha told him that the doctors said that she had amnesia from the beating and that her memory would return, but couldn't tell her when. The doctors told her that it would come back slowly and for her not to try to force it or it would repress itself. She also told Philip about the dream and how she was so close to remembering who the person was, but when it came time to see his face, she always woke up.

Philip had done some research for a company that was trying to find a way to open the mind so that people with amnesia could remember, but the findings were all the same. The mind protected itself until the person was physically and mentally well enough to deal with the memories that were suppressed. Philip was quite amazed how the body worked, that it could do such a thing. He also knew that, in some circumstances, it could be deadly for someone to remember. It was getting late and he knew that he should go. If he didn't leave now, he never would. Talking to Stasha tonight was what they both should have done over the two weeks they had in Montreal. He realized that trying to hide himself from this woman was almost the biggest mistake that he could have done. After talking to her, he knew that, even if she tried, she could never be like the other women that he dated. She had a big heart.

Going to the door, Philip slipped his arms around Stasha's waist. He looked down at her lips, seeing how tantalizing they were and knew that there was no way he was going to leave until he had a taste of them once more. As their lips touched, Philip could taste the wine that remained on her's and deepened the kiss.

Stasha's head began to swirl and never knew a kiss could affect her quite like this. If Philip wasn't holding on to her, she knew that she would have fallen because her legs felt like Jell-O. Philip pulled away slowly and could see her eyes were glazed and felt good that he could get this reaction from her because he knew he felt the same. Letting her go was something that he didn't want to do, but knew that he better leave now. He promised himself that there would be plenty of time to take it farther in the future. Opening the door, he turned to wish her a good night and to remind her to lock the door when he left. Looking at her with her lips swollen from the kiss they shared was almost enough to make him stay. And by the look of her, it wouldn't have take much to convince her. Stasha was thinking the same thing, but wanted him to make the choice. As he walked out the door, she knew his answer and let it be. She would never beg a man to be with her. After Eric, she had promised herself that she would never do so again. As Philip walked to the elevator, he was determined to keep her safe and he wanted to call *Monsieur* Monteau to find out what really happened.

CHAPTER 8

Philip drove back to his place and rode the elevator up to his apartment. As the elevator opened, he started to compare his place to Stasha's. While he spent thousands of dollars for the interior designer to make the place look contemporary, Stasha's place felt like home the moment he walked in. Philip looked around at the place, which by anyone's standards was spectacular, but felt suddenly cold to him. The colors were all masculine and the dark wood that was supposed to complement the colors of the walls seemed very dark to him now. Putting his jacket away and walking over to the bar, he grabbed himself a beer out of the bar fridge and walked over to the window. He had to admit that the view was perfect though. Living on Park Avenue in New York was one of the things he worked very hard for. He remembered how he told his grandfather about his dreams and why he worked so hard to understand everything. After that talk, his grandfather seemed to push him harder, and Philip was glad he did. Everyone around him, except his family, thought that it was just handed over after his grandfather died, but that was not the case. Looking out over Central Park, Philip remembered how his grandfather had always said to him, "Philip, if you want this company, you will have to prove that you're capable of running it; knowing how it works is very important. If you do not know how your company works, there are always people in a company that will try to take it away. Only a man who knows his company inside out will be the one still holding it in the end. I will not hand it over to you until you can prove to me that I picked the right man for the tremendous job of keeping it going. This has been in my family for years and I do not want someone who will throw it away because he never wanted to learn."

Philip knew that his grandfather loved him very much, but he was not a stupid man. Philip proved to his grandfather that his choice was the right one and got the opportunity to work alongside him for many years. Philip learned so much from him, not only how to be the man who owned one of the largest laboratories in the world, but to be able to work alongside the employees that he maintained. His grandfather had received respect from his employees for making them feel equal and not just a worker; he passed that trait over to Philip. Philip knew that if it wasn't for his employees he would not have a company. Stepping back from the window, he remembered showing his grandfather the place when he bought it. His grandfather laughed and asked him why a single man would need a place so big and one with two baths and five bedrooms. Grandfather Demonde also showed Philip to look to the future and knew that, one day; this place would be home to his great-grandchildren. Philip liked how everything was open concept and also the large staircase that led to the bedrooms above. The living room had a step down with a large gas fireplace. The mantle over the fireplace held pictures of his parents and sister and her children. Philip hoped that one day he would have pictures of his own children there. Family was very important to him. At thirty- five, he knew that if he was going to have a large family he would need to find someone soon.

Walking into the kitchen, he grabbed some almonds from the jar that was kept on the counter and walked back to the living room and sat down on the couch. He went over everything that Stasha had told him. He was worried that whoever did that to her three years ago might try again if it was the project they were after, and Philip had no doubt that it was the reason she was beaten. He knew that the next thing he had to do was talk to *Monsieur* Monteau, since he was there the whole time that Stasha was in the hospital. Looking at the clock, he realized that it was well after eleven now and it would have to wait until tomorrow. He would call him first thing. The project was important to Stasha and to him, not just from the business point, but how much it meant to her personally. He wanted to make sure that both stayed safe.

Getting up from the couch, Philip put his bottle away and walked up the stairs to his bedroom, wishing that she was here too. The bedroom was big, but felt very lonely. He had never spent a night with a woman here, but always preferred to stay at her place. He always felt that the woman that he brought home to stay would be the one who stayed forever. After taking off his clothes, he laid them over the chair; he knew that Stella would have them cleaned and put back in place tomorrow. Stella had been his grandfather's maid for ten years before he died and Philip had hired her right after. Stella had rules and Philip didn't mind following them because she always knew how to keep a house and she always did those little extras that any other person would say was not part of their job. Climbing into bed, Philip thought back to the evening with Stasha and the kiss that they shared before he left. The attraction was there and most of his body had felt it too. After talking to her, he was determined to find out more about her. On that thought, he fell asleep.

Philip arrived at work just after eight and started looking over the paperwork that he signed yesterday with Tom. His lawyer, Brad Elliott, was coming in at eleven to make sure that everything was in the correct place for the merge to go through. The contract stipulated that either party would not lose any shares to each other, but would split the financial gain that came from any project they worked on together. It was a sweet deal because Philip didn't like the idea that his company would be in the hands of someone else to take over, so he arranged for it to be strongly stipulated in a way that Magna would in no terms receive any part of Tantum and vice versa. Brad made sure that the contract was solid, and now he would make sure that everything was in place to have it registered. Brad was one of the best corporate lawyers around. When Philip hired him, he knew that he was in good hands. Both men had become friends over the years and Philip trusted Brad like a brother.

When Jason announced that Brad was here, Philip asked him to show Brad in. Jason was Philip's assistant for the last ten years and he was very efficient in his job. Philip hired a man because every woman that he interviewed for the position seemed to imply that they could do more for him than just work. Philip didn't want to have to deal with a secretary that was willing to do side jobs. When he told his grandfather why he hired a man, his grandfather just laughed and told him that it was a smart idea.

Brad came in and sat in the chair across from Philip. Jason came in with two coffees and some muffins on a platter. Philip thanked him and told him to hold his calls unless it was an emergency. Jason knew that if Philip's family called he was to put them through and Philip would then tell them he would call them back. He always made sure that Philip received the messages right away. Inside the office, Brad reached for a muffin and took a bite. Philip knew as he took a sip of his coffee that Brad would enjoy the muffin before work got started. Like Philip, Brad was a big man, but with regular exercise he stayed quite fit. Brad was a very good looking guy and, on more than one occasion, both of them would be swamped with women around them when they went out together. Brad loved all types of women: big, small, skinny, or plump, because he said that God created all women to be perfect in any size. He never used them, but loved the attention he would gain from them. After finishing his muffin, he went to wash his hands in the washroom just off the office. Coming back, he reached for his briefcase and took out the papers that he had received from Tom Belinger's lawyer yesterday.

"Everything is a go. All the papers are signed, and I can have this registered this afternoon," Brad told him. "This is the best deal that you have ever made and it will mean more business in more sectors of the world for us. The places that we haven't been able to touch, like the Middle East, we have clearance now because Magna already does and that can only widen the horizon for us. With their connections, we will be able to add laboratories in their areas. Tom's lawyer and I went through everything yesterday and I'm prepared to file them this afternoon." Brad couldn't wait to get this under way. Things could only go up from here for them now. "So how is everyone at home?" Brad asked. A few times, Brad had accompanied Philip back to Montreal and loved the city. Philip's family had welcomed him with open arms and Philip's mom was the best. She fussed over him as if he was one of her own. They had a fair sized home and, even though they did well in the shipping business, they treated people all the same. They were good people. He liked them all.

"Everyone is very well. I went to the wedding of a very good friend of theirs, and actually met a beautiful woman to boot."

At the mention of a beautiful woman, Brad's attention was caught. Philip had to laugh because he knew that, once he said that, Brad would want to know who she was. "So tell me, buddy, who would this beautiful woman be?" Brad asked, hoping that this one would at least be normal. The other women that Phil went out with were only after his money and when Brad had the chance to have a little chat with them and informed them that even if they did get to the alter with Philip, there was an iron clad prenuptial that would be needed to be signed before the wedding. Plus, he always hinted that he liked to do background checks on people that might in any way hurt his friend. Most of the time, the relationships seemed to dwindle down to nothing.

Philip knew that Brad did this and why he did it. Philip liked the idea that his buddy was looking out for him. "Yes, I believe you know her. Her name is Stasha Monteau and it was her father that had gotten married." Philip filled Brad in on the rest. He told him how they had gotten to know each other and how he had kept his last name from her. He also filled him in on the meeting and the slap that followed. "I had to clear things up with her because, Brad, I have never felt like this. We went on dates and I didn't have to worry that she was just there because of my money. I really got to know the real her and she did the same."

Brad could tell that Philip was caught. "Are you telling me that you are attracted to the same woman that you will be working very closely with over the next few months?" Brad asked astonished. Philip never got involved with a co-worker. Brad thought that he had better get started on a background check on Miss. Monteau. He had to watch Phil's back.

Philip knew that look that passed over his friend's face. "Save your time on that background check my friend. Stasha has her own money and both her dad and she have been in a partnership in a new venture that we actually took part in the last time we were in Montreal."

Brad asked Philip what that would have been, with a smile on his face. "Stasha and her father own "Mon Petite", the one with the comedy club next door." Brad whistled because that was one of the classiest places he had ever been to, and the comedy club was the only one he went to that kept it going for a full evening. Philip also informed him that Stasha had shares in the company that her father owned and would receive the rest on his death. "So, Brad, I would say that Miss Monteau is actually my equal or pretty close. I know that she would not go after me for my money when she tried so hard to show that she doesn't have any, even though she is almost as rich as I am. She has worked hard for everything, too, and I have great respect for that."

Brad smiled and said, "So, you did a background check of your own before you got involved with this deal and found out some information?"

Philip nodded. "You know me; don't jump into the fire if you're going to get burned."

"Well, when do I get to meet this beautiful woman that you seem so caught up in?"

At that precise moment, Jason buzzed the office and told Philip that a Miss Monteau was in the reception area and would like to speak with him. Philip told Jason to bring her in. "I guess you won't have to wait too long. Be on your best behavior Brad." Just as Philip finished speaking to Brad, the door opened. Philip smiled because he couldn't wait to see the reaction on Brad's face. Thanking Jason as she walked through the door he was holding for her, smiling, she made her way over to Philip. Kissing him on both cheeks, she looked at him and said hello. Confused why he had a silly grin on his face, she turned to see what he was looking at. It was then that she noticed that they were not the only two people in the room. She smiled at Brad and hoped that he would say something soon because he was making her feel uncomfortable.

"Stasha, may I introduce you to one of my best friends, Brad Elliott. Brad why don't you close your mouth long enough to say hello to Stasha. Brad shook himself. He had seen a lot of beautiful women in his lifetime, but never one as beautiful as her. Stasha wore cream silk pants and a cream sweater with a light tan belt that seemed to hug her hips. Her hair was also left down and the highlights shimmered in the light. She looked very slim in cream and her complexion seemed softer with those colors.

Stasha tried to wear very little make up, but the way it was applied brought out the beauty in her face. When she gave Brad a smile and said hello, he thought that he just stopped breathing. "How are you Mr. Elliott? Did I interrupt something? If so, I could come back later."

Philip said they were through and Brad was just leaving.

"I wondered if you were free for lunch, but if you're busy, then how about stopping in for supper this evening?" Stasha asked. Last night, they talked so much and she really enjoyed it. She also wanted to let Philip know that she did know how to cook, and prove it to him. She knew that, once they started on the project, there would be little time to socialize.

Philip escorted Brad to the door. As Brad was leaving, he asked Philip, "Please tell me that she has a sister!" Philip laughed and told Brad that he would call him later that afternoon to see how it all went. Walking over to Stasha, he put his arms around her and leaned down for a kiss. As soon as his lips touched hers, sparks seemed to just bounce of them. After pulling away before things got to out of control, he asked her, "So, you came all this way to have lunch with me?" After her nod, he said, "So, if I go to lunch with you, does that mean that supper is out or do I get both?"

Stasha liked the game he was playing and thought a little flirting could be called for. "Well, Mr. Demonde, I could make you choose one over the other, but I cannot be so mean. I have a proposition for you. You take me to lunch and I'll cook for you tonight."

Philip knew that was an offer he was going to take. With a smile, he walked her to the door and opened it for her. Walking out to the reception area, he told Jason that he would be taking Miss Monteau to lunch and would be back in about an hour or so.

Jason thought that Philip was a lucky guy. When Miss Monteau walked in and asked to see Philip, at first he thought that she was another one of those women that seemed to latch themselves onto him, but when she asked very business-like, but very politely if Mr. Demonde was available, Jason knew that she was not like the others. She didn't talk down to him, but rather talked to him and made him feel important. "Do you need these papers ready to be signed when you get back?"

Philip knew that Jason would work through lunch to have them ready and didn't like any of the employees missing lunch. "No, Jason, take lunch and then when you get back start on them and I'll sign them when they're done. If you need to reach me I have my cell."

He had not seen Philip look that way at a woman before, and knew that a certain bug had caught him.

As the elevator doors closed, Philip grabbed Stasha in his arms and gave her a kiss that he had wanted to give her ever since she walked in his office. It left both of them breathless by the time they reached the lobby. "There is a little restaurant just down the street that has the best sandwiches and salads. Is it ok if we just walk there, it's not too far?" Stasha told him it would be fine.

Once they reached the restaurant, Stasha realized that it wasn't an expensive place. They sat themselves down at a table and waited for the waitress to take their order. Stasha was glad that she made the decision to ask him to lunch and worried that he may have been to busy to go. She was happy that he had decided to take her to lunch, and then tonight he would come for supper. Stasha had never felt like this before and, after last night, thought it was about time she was happy with someone; after all, they did have a lot in common. Secretly, she hoped that he wouldn't turn in to an Eric, but she was not going to dwell on it and planned to enjoy what they had.

The waitress took their order. Philip ordered a clubhouse sandwich, a large Greek salad, and an iced tea. Stasha passed on the sandwich and ordered the soup of the day, which was vegetable and a lunch sized salad with a club soda and lemon. Philip was glad that his little test passed with flying colors. Stasha didn't turn up her nose at the place like a lot of other women did when he brought them here and ended up taking them somewhere else because of the reaction he received. Once the waitress came with their food, they both dived in right away. They talked about work and the little things they needed to accomplish before the day was over.

After finishing lunch, Stasha thanked the waitress for the very good food and service; that little gesture pleased Philip more. The waitress was happy also because she had a smile on her face when they left. Philip slipped his hand in hers and they strolled back to his office.

"Thank you for lunch; I had a great time and liked that place. It was small, but very clean and the food was very good. I think that my soup must have been homemade because of the unique flavor."

Philip couldn't help but smile. That restaurant was his and his grandfather's favorite place to go for lunch. He remembered his grandfather telling him, "See this small place; they make the best food here. Always have, that's why I have been coming here for over forty years. These people do what they have to, to make ends meet, and they are always nice to you when you walk in the door. It's people who think their too good for a place like this, who are actually missing the finer things in life. Remember, money doesn't make you who you are, the heart inside you does." He told Stasha about what his grandfather said to him the first day he brought him to the restaurant and how the times spent there meant to both of them.

Stasha told him that his grandfather had good taste and that he was a very smart man too. As they approached his building, Philip kissed her once more before she went back to work. After he kissed her, she told him that if he kept doing that she would never be able to work this afternoon and that would mean that she would never make it home in time to make supper for him. They agreed that he would come over about seven-thirty.

Philip hailed a cab for her and placed her inside and promised to see her later. Philip walked into his office and Jason asked how his lunch was. Jason had his answer. Philip was in love, big time. As he closed the door, Philip walked over to his desk and sat down. He wanted to talk to *Monsieur* Monteau about Stasha. Picking up the phone, he asked Jason to dial the number and if he could put him through. A few minutes went by and Jason buzzed in to tell him that Mr. Monteau would be on the line in a minute. Philip picked up the phone and waited.

Marcel came on the line, "Hello Philip, how is the cheek?" he said with a chuckle.

"Well sir, it stung for a minute, but doing fine now. Stasha and I straightened everything out last night and we actually talked about a lot of things."

Marcel wondered if Stasha told him about the incident and had his answer in the next breath.

"*Monsieur,* I have to ask you about what happened to her three years ago?" Marcel knew how much it hurt talking about seeing his child lying in the hospital and how he stayed through the whole ordeal. He also told Philip that he had men in place to always keep her safe. Philip had told him that they were not hiding too well. When he left her apartment last night he had seen one of them outside.

Marcel was alarmed at this news because the men he hired were the best and there was no way that Philip would have spotted one of them. Marcel told him that he would call him right back.

Philip hung up the phone and wondered who the guy was that had been watching Stasha's place last night. He thought that maybe it was someone waiting for someone else in the building, but now he had a feeling that it wasn't.

The phone rang and Marcel was back on the line. "I just got in touch with my main guy there and they tell me that they have been watching this guy very closely, but when they get to close, he seems to take off. They have made sure that Stasha has been watched around the clock and will not let anyone get too close to do that to her again."

Philip asked Marcel how he was able to get up to her apartment last night without being stopped.

Marcel explained that going into the business with her, Marcel sent a picture to them so they would know what he looked like. "I have known your family for along time and I trust you with my daughter."

Philip thought that this would be a good time to tell him. "Sir, I have the utmost respect for your daughter and I would like to let you know that I plan to see her out of work also."

Marcel sat at his desk and had a huge grin on his face. He was very happy that Philip and his daughter would be together. Marcel knew his grandfather and knew that he instilled very good values in his grandson's head. Stasha couldn't have found a better man. "I hope that you will respect her, Philip. She is very special to me and I don't want her to be hurt. If this is a game, then the game stops now. If you care for her, then I give you permission to date my daughter."

Philip knew that Stasha was old enough to date him without her father's permission, but it felt good asking for it anyway. Now, Marcel and Philip would be able to work together to make sure she stayed safe. Hanging up the phone, Philip started on some of the work he needed to do after lunch and made sure that he would have plenty of time to get home to shower.

Stasha went back to the office after lunch with a spring in her step. As she went into her office, Tara commented that wherever she went to lunch, she would have to tell her. Stasha laughed and told her about the restaurant and how things went. She kept the kiss to herself. It was a secret that she thought back to for the rest of the day. She had a meeting with Tom later in the afternoon about the small projects that were on the go. He told her how proud he was of her with the way she handled the presentation yesterday. Stasha told him what had transpired in Montreal and how she didn't know that Philip was the same person that she had met while away.

Tom finally understood why she was so tense yesterday. "I hope that you two resolved everything because we need his company to get your project off the ground. His labs are the only ones that have the equipment to do what is needed." Stasha understood where Tom was going and reassured him that everything was fine. She told him how they had talked last night and everything was ok.

Tom knew that something else was going on, but he would not interfere as long as it did not cause any problems with the companies.

By the time Stasha got back to her office, it was almost four o'clock and she wanted to hit the market on the way home. Just as she was getting her coat on, her phone rang. Tara was not at her desk so the call transferred over to her. Stasha picked it up and said "Hello, Stasha Monteau." On the other end, Stasha heard a rough voice come on. "The research that you're working on should be dead, just like you." Stasha held the phone so hard and couldn't seem to breathe; even though the connection was broken, she couldn't seem to put the phone down. Tara walked in and saw how white she was and asked her if she was alright.

At the same time, Philip and Tom were walking down the hall towards her office. Philip went home early and thought that he would pick her up from work and take her home. As they both walked into her office, they saw Tara grabbing the phone out of her hand and helping her to sit down. Tom rushed over to her, as did Philip. She was white as a sheet.

"What happened to her?" Philip asked Tara.

"I don't know. I had to go and get more paper for my computer and I came back and she was just standing there."

Stasha seemed to snap out of it and told Tom, Philip, and Tara about the phone call. Tom was angry that someone would call her and say such a thing. Philip knew he needed to call Marcel and tell him what just took place.

"The funny thing, Tom, is that I have heard that voice before, but I just can't seem to remember where."

Philip took Tara aside and asked her where he could go to get better reception on his cell. She told him the boardroom because it had no interference there. Philip walked over to Stasha and told her that he would be back in a minute and not to leave without him. She nodded as she accepted a glass of water from Tara.

In the boardroom, Philip dialed Marcel. "Hello Marcel, this is Philip. I just came to pick Stasha up and we have had an incident. I would like you to call your guys and tell them that whoever beat her up three years ago may have just called her.

Marcel didn't like to hear this. After so long, he thought that the creep would have given up. "Thanks for calling. How is she?" Marcel wished he was there.

"Don't worry, sir, I will make sure that nothing happens to her. You can reach me at this number night or day."

After Marcel got off the phone with Philip, he phoned the person in charge of making sure that nothing happened to Stasha. As the phone was answered, Marcel said, "What the hell is happening there? I just got a call that my daughter was threatened on the phone not ten minutes ago. Also, did you find out who that guy is that is watching her from outside her own building yet!"

Ted knew that Marcel was mad. Ted would be mad to if his daughter looked like Stasha after the guy got finished with her. Ted told him that they had brought in a couple more guys to make sure that no harm came to her.

"Well, I hope that these guys are good because I pay a lot of money to make sure she stays alive and healthy," Marcel said. Ted knew that Marcel paid them well and he wasn't about to make his customer sorry that he had picked him. "Philip will be watching Stasha more and I'm glad that he is going to be there. He is bringing her home and I want you to make sure that nobody is out there watching her. This guy is going to make a slip and I want you to make sure that you're there when it happens. I want this guy, Ted. I want him to be sorry for what he did to my daughter three years ago."

Ted talked to his guys and informed them what had happened. Ted knew that the last three years had ended; now the real work would begin.

CHAPTER 9

Philip got Stasha in his car and went around to get in the other side. She was a little shaken, but, otherwise, ok.

"Philip since you are bringing me home, could you please stop at the market because I need to pick up some things for supper."

Philip really just wanted to get her home, but the look in her eyes made him turn the car towards the market. Philip vowed that he would not let anything happen to her. At the market, Stasha picked out the salmon that she planned to grill and some fresh greens for a salad. Then, she went over to the fruit and picked out some strawberries and also some semi-sweet chocolate. Then she had Philip drive her to pick up some wine. When she was done, he was glad when they pulled up to her building. As Philip went to get the packages out of the car, Stasha went over to help.

"It's ok, I've got them." Philip was trying to keep the packages in his arms without them falling, but Stasha insisted that she would help. As they went up the stairs, the door man opened the door. "Hello Ted, how is the family?"

"Just fine, Miss Monteau, thank you for asking. How was work today?" Stasha liked Ted. He always had a nice thing to say to her and had a kind face. Philip heard him ask about her day and alarms were going off. Going past Ted, Philip was surprised when he said, "And a good evening to you too, Mr. Demonde."

Philip looked at him and knew that he was one of Marcel's men. It was a smart idea to have one of them directly at the door because he would see exactly who came and went. Philip made a mental note to talk to Ted when he got the chance. Going up the elevator, he could see that Stasha's color was back and she didn't seem to be as shaken as she was earlier. Going into the apartment Philip did a quick sweep of the place with his eyes and everything looked in order. They both brought everything Stasha bought into the kitchen.

"Could you please take my coat and put it into the closet, and I will get started on this supper I promised you."

Philip took both their coats and hung them up. Walking over to the fireplace, he put a small fire on and went back into the kitchen to help. "Are you sure you're ok?" he asked. Looking at her now, anyone would think that nothing had happened.

"Yes, I'm fine. It just shocked me, that's all. I know I've heard that voice before, but can't recall where. It was a little muffled, but still, it sounded familiar."

Philip wondered why someone would say that particular thing though. "Stasha, let me help you with something." Philip needed to keep busy.

"No, I promised you a supper since you took me for lunch today. You could go and pour us a drink. I think I could use one; you look like you could use one also."

Philip went over to the bar and poured her a glass of wine and grabbed himself a beer. Bringing the wine into the kitchen, he handed it over to her and watched her take a sip. He couldn't believe that here he was with this beautiful woman and how smart she was, but so down to earth. All the best qualities all rolled up in one, and he was standing right here taking it all in. Philip set the table and Stasha brought in the food.

She loved to cook, as long as it wasn't for one. She decided to serve grilled salmon, asparagus tips with a cream wine sauce, and baked potatoes with sour cream and chives. In the kitchen, she had her chocolate fondue, slowly melting the chocolate. Chocolate covered strawberries were her favorite and she thought that it was a very romantic pass time. She had never had the chance to try it, but she had tasted them in restaurants. Plus, she wouldn't mind having a romantic evening with Philip. He made her comfortable and she wasn't going to waste a minute of it. As they sat and ate supper, they talked about the other things that happened at work after their lunch together. Philip told her how everything was registered for both companies and that they could start the project at the beginning of next week. She raised her glass and he raised his beer in salute to their accomplishments.

Stasha was so happy. She had waited so long and the research seemed endless. Now, they could start putting everything together.

After supper was finished, Philip and Stasha cleared the table and cleaned up the kitchen. It wasn't so bad, Philip thought, because she was the kind of cook that cleaned as she went. Stasha arranged a platter with strawberries, cheeses and some crackers. The chocolate fondue was set in the middle. Carrying it out and placing it on the table, she picked up her wine and sat back on the couch. Philip thought how nice everything was and could picture long nights in front of the fire with this woman. Philip put his arm around Stasha and she cuddled into the crook of his arm. They sat there and just immersed themselves in the quietness around them.

Stasha looked up at Philip; as she did he looked down at her. Ever so slowly, he moved towards those luscious lips. As they touched, heat seemed to pour through him. Stasha felt herself getting warm and wanted to have more. Opening her mouth slightly was all the invitation that Philip needed. He wrapped his arms around her and pulled her on his lap. He deepened the kiss, and then brought his lips so softly down her neck, leaving a hot trail to her collarbone. Stasha didn't want him to stop and urged him on. Philip would not have been able to stop if he wanted to. Gathering her in his arms, he picked her up and walked towards the bedroom. Walking towards the bed, he gently laid her down and lowered himself down beside her. Philip looked at her and could see that her eyes were glazed with passion. Slowly, he caressed her neck and let his hand trail down over her breast. He could feel her nipples peak at the slightest touch.

Stasha watched him as he touched her and knew that the things she had been thinking about Philip over the last few days were going to be fulfilled. She was going to take in every moment that he offered her. As Philip passed each button on her shirt, he undid them one by one. Gently, he moved her shirt over, and then caressed the swells of each breast, admiring the fullest of each. Stasha pulled him down so she could taste his lips and ran her fingers through his thick hair.

As the kiss broke, Philip asked her, "Are you sure?" With the nod of acceptance from Stasha, he gently pulled her to her feet. Standing in front of him, Stasha put her hands on his chest and felt how hard it was. She started to undo the buttons of his shirt; when she completed that task, she took it off and let it fall to the floor. Placing her hands on his chest, she could feel how hot his skin was to the touch. She looked up at him for a moment, and then ducked her head and kissed his chest. She could feel the slightest ripple go through him and felt a power she had never experienced before.

As Stasha kissed him, Philip had the same feelings go through him. There was never a woman who made him feel what Stasha did with just one small move. He didn't know how long he could endure this torture, but stood still while Stasha continued. When he thought he would explode, he put his fingers under her chin to have her face him, and then kissed her again. At this point, they made short order of removing their clothes and joined each other on the bed. Philip laid down beside her and caressed every part his eyes could see. He knew that he was falling fast. He bent his head and took one nipple into his mouth and suckled so gently that Stasha thought that she would not be able to take much more. Then, he moved to the other to give it the same attention.

Stasha ran her hands down his back and felt the muscles harden under her palms. Reaching between them, she slowly let her hand trail down, giving him the same attention. Gathering his erection in her hand, she caressed it with the same slowness that Philip paid to her breast. At this point, Philip knew that he would not be able to hold on. He moved on top of her. Philip looked down at Stasha with such feelings in his eyes and lifted her hips slightly. At that moment, Philip plunged himself all the way in. Even though he knew that Stasha was not a virgin, he could tell that she had not been intimate in a while because she was so tight. He waited until she started to relax and grew accustomed to his size.

Stasha had never realized that a man could be so big. She felt the tightness, but it was starting to recede and she could feel the stirrings of other feelings overwhelming her. Stasha kissed Philip with every feeling she had inside her, and started to move her hips.

Philip wanted to take things slow, but he couldn't hold back. He gave himself up to the feelings that rushed forward. They came in a great climax, both yelling out at the same time. Afterward, Philip still laying on Stasha, tried to get his breath back. After a few minutes, he lifted himself off her and laid on his side. As Philip looked over, Stasha still had her eyes closed and Philip could see a single tear run down her face. Leaning over her, he wiped the tear away with his finger and gathered her close. "Oh baby, I didn't mean to hurt you. You have to believe that. I couldn't hold on anymore, but please believe me that I wouldn't hurt you for the world." Philip hated that he did this to her. He lost all conscious thought as things progressed.

Stasha opened her eyes and couldn't believe that, even though he lay beside her, she still had the feeling of her climax still running through her. She never in her life had experienced a feeling like that, and to have it continue was beyond her. She suddenly realized that Philip had a concerned look on his face, and she smiled at him. Stasha asked him what was wrong and what he was apologizing for. She told him that she had never experienced such love making and how great it had been.

Philip blew out the breath he was holding and sank back onto the bed and gathered her in his arms. "I'm so sorry for going so fast with you the first time, but I promise you that I will take it much slower the next time." Philip put actions to his words and took it slower. When they were done the second time, Stasha was amazed that lovemaking could be done so soon after finishing the first time and that a woman could have multiple orgasms. Eric had been the only one she had been with and he would do what he wanted, and then fall asleep right after. Philip showed her what she had been missing all those years. Getting out of bed, she decided to take a shower.

As she got up, Philip followed. As they stepped into the shower, Philip showed Stasha that the shower could be used for other things. Stasha thought after they were finished that she would never look at that shower again the same way. Philip had put his pants back on, but left his chest bare. Stasha put on her robe and they both went out into the living room.

Stasha went over to the bar and got a beer for Philip, but he decided to have a glass of wine with her. Since they had worked up an appetite, they both started dipping the strawberries in the smooth chocolate. As they sat there in front of the fire, Stasha told Philip that she had only been with one person before him and how she never thought of how much she had missed out on.

At this, Philip laughed out loud. In a way, he felt sorry for her because he thought every woman should experience just as much as the man. Philip knew that as long as they were together, he would make sure that she received as much or more out of each experience, and he planned on a lot more of them. Philip had never in his life felt this good. Sitting on the couch, Stasha sat cuddled up to Philip's side, and he had his arm wrapped around her. He told her how he called her father that afternoon and how her father gave him permission to date her.

"You do know that I'm of age, don't you? There was no need to do that, but I know that you made my father happy. That was really nice of you." Stasha's feelings deepened in that one gesture for Philip because her father meant everything to her and she knew that Marcel would admire that sort of trait in a man. "You know that you have just committed yourself to trips with me back to Montreal because, if I go home without you, my father is going to send me back to get you." Philip laughed because he could see Marcel doing just that.

"Stasha, remember that my family also lives there, so really, we will be killing two birds with one stone. You see, once my family knows we're involved, I'm in the same boat as you. My mother is going to be so happy. She had commented on what a nice girl you were at the wedding; and my mother was the one who had the picnic basket done up the day we went for a drive."

Stasha laughed at this and reminded herself to thank his mother when she saw her next. It had been a long day for both of them. Stasha yawned. Philip told her that he should get going; hopefully wishing that she would ask him to stay. Stasha didn't disappoint him. They walked back to the bedroom and fell asleep in each others arms.

The next morning, the alarm clock went off and Stasha stretched and felt muscles that she never knew existed. There was soreness between her legs and she remembered how it came to be. After they fell asleep last night, Philip had woken her up in the middle of the night and made love to her again. She looked to the other side of the bed and realized that it was empty. Philip must have gone early. Stasha knew that today was like any other day, and that work would be waiting for her. She got out of bed and went to have a shower. Turning the hot water on, she stepped in and let the water work out some of the soreness from her body. She never thought that a person could do such things in the shower that Philip proved could be done. She turned her thoughts back to the shower and quickly washed. Stepping out and wrapping a towel around her, she went into the bedroom to get dress. After looking at herself, she realized her skin had a certain glow to it, smiling, she made her way to the kitchen. Instead of Mary being the one in the kitchen, Philip sat at the table. He must have had a shower earlier because he was dressed.

Looking up, he smiled at her. "I hope you don't mind, but I'm an early riser and thought you would like a cup of coffee when you got up." Philip pulled out the chair for her and Stasha sat down. Philip went over to the coffee pot and poured her a cup.

Stasha accepted the cup and took a sip. It tasted so good and she wondered why her coffee didn't taste as good.

"How do you want your eggs?" Philip asked as he went to the fridge and pulled out a couple of eggs and a plate of fresh cut fruit. Placing the fruit on the table, he leaned down and kissed her. Turning to the stove, he started to make them breakfast.

"I didn't know you could cook," Stasha said. She was always the one to cook for people. She had never had anyone cook for her, not even Franny. The only time she didn't cook was when she went home. Monique was a great cook and her dad's rounding belly was proof. Philip laughed and told her that no one left his mother's house without knowing how to cook. He told her that his mother was afraid they would starve when they went to university. Stasha smiled and remembered when her father made them take a cooking class when she was in high school.

As Philip put the plate in front of Stasha, he could see that she was surprised. He had made the fixings for omelets while she slept and waited for her to get up. Stasha took a bite and was surprised at how good it tasted.

"I hope you don't mind that I raided your fridge, but after last night I thought we should both have a good breakfast before going to work," Philip told her.

Stasha was still wondering how she ever became so lucky to find this man and if it was a dream than she wanted to sleep forever. "If this is a sample of what you can do in the kitchen, then you can raid my cupboards or fridge anytime." Stasha insisted that, since he cooked, she would clean up. After she was done, Philip told her that he would drop her off at work and then run home to change. Before Stasha could go through the door, Philip kissed her.

"Have I told you how beautiful you are today?" Philip said.

"If you keep up this kind of talk, Mr. Demonde, I may never get to work," Stasha told him with a sly smile on her face. Philip patted her bottom as she went through the door.

CHAPTER 10

The week flew by and Stasha had agreed to meet Franny for lunch. They met at a restaurant not too far from Stasha's work. Franny was already there when she arrived. Ordering a soda with lemon and a Greek salad, she asked Franny how she was.

"Work has been so busy. I'm still doing some double shifts. I would like to get home to see Mom and Dad soon. Mom told me that Marie is expecting again."

Franny, Stasha knew, had wanted to go to the wedding so that she would have time to spend with the family. "Franny do you think that you could get the Canada Day weekend off? I know that the Fourth of July is a big holiday in the States, but you've worked so much overtime, do you think that they might give you the time off? This way, the three of us could go home together and see everyone."

Franny didn't miss a beat. "Wait a minute, who is the three of us?" she asked.

Stasha had waited all week to tell Franny about Philip. "Well, you know that I met someone when I went home. Well, we have been seeing each other and, Franny, I can't tell you how much I missed out on when I was with Eric!" She laughed. Stasha had already told her about what happened when she got back from Montreal, and then told her what happened at the meeting. Franny laughed when she heard how Stasha slapped him. Stasha was not a person to use physical means on anyone. Stasha didn't go into detail, but told her how wonderful the evening was they spent together. "Eric knows shit about lovemaking!" Stasha blurted out, which sent Franny laughing so hard that she was holding her stomach and tears were coming down her cheeks. Stasha started to laugh too. Franny was the only one who knew that Eric had been her first.

"Well, when do I get to meet this man of yours?" Franny asked.

"As soon as you get some time off. Franny, ask for the holiday off and we can go home and have some fun." Stasha missed the old days of being around Franny's whole family. She had seen them at the wedding, but, with so many things to take care of, she didn't get to spend that much time with them.

"Okay, I'll ask, but no promises. Though, it would be nice to be able to spend Canada Day with my family. I'll ask when I get back and phone you with the answer."

Getting back to the office, Tara had her schedule for the rest of the day on her desk. Stasha had to meet with the manufacturing company that wanted to build the handheld device that would hopefully be used by millions of people. Tara walked in with some tea for both of them.

"You have enough time for this, and then you have to go to Tantum to see the outlines for the device. Mr. Arnold called and wants you to see the details that he has finished."

Stasha was waiting for him to call her. This was the first step, and then it would be transferred to Philip's labs to be worked on. Stasha sat in her chair and sipped her tea. It felt good getting together with Franny. They had caught up on things, since Stasha was either at work or with Philip most of the time. She hoped that Franny would call her later and tell her that she could go with them to Montreal. Stasha couldn't wait for Philip to meet Franny's family, which she considered her own. Handing Tara her cup, she gathered her papers and went to see Mr. Arnold.

Walking by Tom's office, she saw that he was just sitting there. "Tom, anything I could help with; I was just on my way to see Mr. Arnold who has some details to go over, but from the sound of everything it looks good."

Tom looked up and smiled. Stasha was the best employee he had ever hired. He remembered a few times when he had gotten caught in a few situations and she stayed late to help him. She had the calmness to break through the problems when he just got more frustrated. "No, I'm fine. Just sitting back and thinking how far we've come. We work well together. Stasha, I was wondering if you might consider taking on a partnership with me. I'm getting old and I won't be able to keep this business going forever on my own. Ida and I were talking last night and she was the one who thought of it, mind you I have thought about it myself a few times, but wasn't ready to give up the reins."

Stasha didn't know what to say. Tom just took the floor right out from under her. She walked in the office and sat in the chair across from him. Stasha loved his wife Ida. She never worked here, but anyone who knew her and Tom knew that she was the other backbone to the company. She was a tiny woman, but was the smartest woman Stasha had ever met. "Well, Tom, you know that I love this company as much as the two of you do and I would be honored to become a partner, on one condition though."

Tom waited for her explanation. He knew that it was the right decision as soon as it left his lips. Ida and he had given everything to the company and, having no children, it was their child. Now they were getting older and wanted to enjoy life a little. Travel and see the world. Sure, they had been on trips, but while away they always worried about the company. As soon as Stasha became his right hand person, it seemed that they didn't worry as much when they went away. Ida brought up the subject a few times, but knew not to allow Tom to think it was her idea. She had to let him believe that it was his. "What would this condition be then?" Tom asked.

Stasha loved Tom and Ida as if they were her own parents. They had always been good to her and Tom always made her work for her position in the company so that others knew she worked for it and didn't sleep her way there. "Well, the condition would be that Ida and yourself take a nice vacation, not just a week mind you, but a whole month and do the things you both have dreamed of doing. I will always make sure that the company will be here for you both. You know that, right, Tom?"

Tom sat back and wished that if Ida and he had ever had a child that she could have been exactly like the woman who sat in front of him. "Well, it's settled then. I will have my lawyer start the paperwork tomorrow," he said with a little emotion in his voice.

Stasha smiled at him because she knew it was a hard thing to give up. "Tom, I promise you that I will never let you regret your decision." She walked over to him and gave him a hug. Turning, she walked out of his office and Tom noticed a spring in her step.

He shook his head with a smile. He was nervous all morning trying to figure out how he was going to approach her with this. Then, she just stepped into his office showing concern and ready to tackle the problem with him. It had been her idea to bring Tantum into the folds, and she was the one who directed the contract so that Tom would not lose any shares in the company. He knew the choice he just made was a good one. He could now relax. He picked up his phone and made the call. "Hi Ed, its Tom. Yes, I just spoke with Stasha and it's a go. Could you please draw up the necessary papers and we will meet at the end of the week to sign them."

Ed knew that Tom had been thinking the decision over and sat with both Ida and Tom to discuss it. Tom and Ida had their Will drawn up at the beginning of the year leaving the company to Stasha, but Ed brought up the idea of a partnership. Ida thought it was a good idea because, in case anything happened to Tom, Stasha would regain control, but Ida would be taken care of.

"How did she take it?" Ed asked.

Tom started to laugh and told Ed how he was so nervous about talking to her. "I'll tell you, Ed, I really didn't know how it was going to go. She tells me that she will accept under one condition." Tom told Ed the rest of it and Ed had to smile. He had met Stasha a few times and liked her. Tom and Ida were very lucky to have someone who cared for them so much and also be a member of their company. Ed naturally had her checked out because of his clients investments and didn't want them to be taken by a sly person. Ed told Tom that he would have everything ready for him and Ida to sign on Friday. After hanging up the phone, Tom called Ida. "Hi honey, everything went fine. I couldn't believe how easy it was. I guess you were right, I was nervous for nothing," Tom told her.

Stasha was in shock all the way to Tantum Labs. She just could believe what had happened. When she saw the look on Tom's face, she thought that something major was wrong. Then, when he asked her to be a partner in the company she loved working for, she thought that she couldn't breath. She didn't want him to think that she couldn't handle herself under pressure. Holding it back and acting casual, Stasha was very surprised with herself. She couldn't wait to tell her dad and Philip what had happened, but she would wait until everything was signed first. People changed their minds and Stasha didn't want Tom to feel pressured.

Arriving in the technical lab at Tantum, Stasha looked around. Magna was getting bigger projects and needed a lab to be able to handle the work.

Mr. Arnold came out of his office and saw Stasha. "Come this way and we'll go over what I have done so far." Motioning her to follow him, they went into a room that was sealed with a number of codes. Only Tom, Philip, Mr. Arnold, and she had the codes to this room. This was where they kept the results to the findings and the diagrams for each project in process. Opening the door, he led her in and both approached the table where he had the diagrams laid out for her to see.

Stasha looked them over as Mr. Arnold explained the structure of the design. This unit was handheld. It would take the blood, do the reading, and show the person who owned the device that either a regular reading had appeared or an irregular reading came up. At this point, the owner would bring it to their doctor who could print out the findings and do the necessary test to see why. He told Stasha that he would be transferring the data over to Philip this afternoon if she approved everything.

Stasha was glad that they had actually gotten this far. She remembered it being an idea so long ago; Eric and Franny, both being in the medical field, told her that it was a great idea. The next day, Stasha started on the research to see if it could be done. Now, it was going to be a reality and she couldn't wait. "Everything looks fine to me; I see that the adjustments we made won't interfere with the model." The first one they had designed had been too bulky. Stasha wanted it to be easy to hold and store. Plus, they also had to work on the program that would enable any doctor to download the program to his or her computer, and then be able to gather the information from the device to get all the readings. Stasha needed the diagrams to be completed first, and then Philip would work with her to get the device and program running. In this type of project, they had to make sure that no mistakes could be made. It had to be as accurate as possible.

Mr. Arnold was pleased that everything they worked on was not done at a rushed pace. He liked to recheck things to make sure that, if a problem did arise, he would know where to look to solve it. He had worked for Philip and his grandfather for almost twenty-five years and enjoyed the freedom and access that Philip gave him on the projects. Maybe that was why they got the best contracts. They were known all over the world for their products and Mr. Arnold was part of most of them. Philip always gave recognition to who deserved it. A few times, companies that competed with Tantum tried to offer him a better deal. He would tell Philip when he was approached and Philip always told him he would have no hard feelings if he left, but would be sad to see him go. Philip made sure that he paid his top people the best wages and Mr. Arnold knew that he would never find the same kind of atmosphere as he would here. When he started working for Tantum, people in the lab called him by his given name, which was Danny. Not Dan or Daniel, but Danny. He was called a nerd all the way through school. He liked to get into projects that were the most difficult and would be able to figure it out. Mr. Demonde hired him to do just that. Mr. Arnold remembered the day Mr. Demonde came down from upstairs to check on a project he was completing and heard someone call him clammy Danny. They always joked around, but Mr. Arnold was the brunt of most of the jokes. Philip's grandfather had gotten so angry at the guys who were calling him that, that he said "If I hear anyone in this company put a co-worker down in that matter again, he will be fired on the spot. You are all here for your experience in your fields and from now on this man will only be address as Mr. Arnold and I mean 'Mr.' for if I hear different, the fire will definitely hit the pan!" Mr. Arnold's admiration for Mr. Demonde had never lessened after that day. He was well respected in the company. The only one who called him Danny now was his wife.

Stasha thanked him for all the long hours he had spent trying to get it completed and went back to Magna. By the time she walked back into her office, it was almost four o'clock. Stasha gathered up her briefcase and coat. Since the accident, Tom would never let her stay past four-thirty. It was nice, in a way, because she arrived home before it got dark in the winter, and in the summer had the chance to go for a walk before dinner. She caught a cab outside and sat back and reflected on what happened today. She thought how someone told her that things always come in threes. First, she met Philip, second, the project was starting to take off, and three, Tom asked her to become a partner. Stasha wished Franny was there to pinch her. She wanted to make sure that it was real.

Stepping out of the cab, she walked up the stairs and greeted Ted "Hi Ted, how was your day?" she asked with a big grin on her face.

"Very good Miss Monteau, and yours?" Ted replied.

"It was the best day, Ted," she replied, as she walked through the door, he held for her. Opening the door to the apartment, Stasha put her coat in the closet and walked over to the bar and poured herself a glass of wine. Bringing it into the kitchen with her, she started supper. She was going to be alone tonight because Philip had a business meeting and he told her that it could take a while. Stasha told him that she had a lot going on and would meet up with him on the weekend. Pulling out a chicken breast and adding some seasoning, she put it in the oven to roast. Taking the fixings out of the fridge for a salad, she tossed it together and would add the chicken to it after it was cooked. She decided to change into some jeans and a sweater. Pulling her hair into a ponytail, she walked back out to the living room. Stasha turned on the television and changed the channel to *Montel*. She enjoyed the subjects that he raised and the conclusions were inspiring. Going back into the kitchen, Stasha took the chicken out and cut it into small pieces. Adding it to the salad, she added the dressing and tossed it. Putting it into a big bowl, she brought her wine and supper to eat in front of the television. Just as she was cleaning up from supper, the phone rang. Franny had just finished work.

Franny told Stasha that she had asked for the time off and the head of nursing had told her that she would put it in for her. She told Stasha how her boss appreciated the over time she put when they were short. Franny had already called her mom and told her that she would be home for Canada Day. She had strict orders to tell Stasha that her family was having a party for the occasion. "Stasha, you remember the great parties Mom threw. She also told me that we have to help." Evette was great. She never left Stasha out of the mix. She had always made sure that Stasha felt like one of the family and when parties were thrown Stasha helped just like everyone else. Franny told her about her day and how there was a new doctor on the scene. Three of the other nurses had dibs on him. Franny wasn't into doctors. She preferred the business suit to the white coat. She never spoke of Eric to Stasha, even though he still worked at the same hospital as she did.

Stasha was so glad that Franny had the time off, and then confided in her about the project and how Tom had asked her to be a partner. "Both happening in the same day, Franny, I thought I was going to faint."

Franny laughed and told Stasha that she knew that it was only a matter of time before Tom came around and saw what a great person he had working for him. Franny was always a great boost for her ego and Stasha did the same for her. Franny told her about the rest of the hospital gossip, there was new stuff everyday to tell her. So, getting it all out in one phone call every few days kept them on the phone for a little while. A half hour later, Franny told Stasha goodbye. Franny was getting a little tired and told Stasha she would call on the weekend.

Stasha went to pour herself another glass of wine and thought how great it was going to be going home for the holiday. She picked up the phone to call her father, but then decided to wait and see what happened with the partnership. It will be nice to tell him about everything in one shot. Stasha turned the news on and caught up on everything that was going on in the city. Looking at the clock, she realized that it was past twelve, so she turned off the TV and went to bed. As she climbed into bed, the phone rang. Reaching over to the phone on her nightstand, she picked it up. In a tired voice, she said "Hello?" No one responded, so Stasha figuring that it was a wrong number and hung it up. The next couple of days were going to be hectic and she needed her sleep. Turning the ringer off on both phones and going back to bed, Stasha knew that they could leave a message still, and then she would get them in the morning.

After taking a shower the next morning, Stasha felt awake again. After having breakfast, she went to get her briefcase that she put beside the couch and realized that she had a message on the machine. It came in at three twenty-three in the morning. After turning the phones off last night, she had slept like the dead. She had been so exhausted that she didn't even hear the machine come on. Pushing the play button, she first heard a raspy noise like static in the background, and then she heard the voice. She could only hear part of what the person was trying to say, "Dead like you," but the first part was missing. She knew that it sounded like the voice that she heard a couple of days ago at the office. She replayed the message trying to see if she could identify the voice. If she could only remember where she had heard it. She shut the machine off and told herself that she was in one of the most secure buildings in New York and it would take someone strong to get past the doormen. Ted and Bill were big guys. Erasing the message, Stasha turned the ringers on and the grabbed her coat and left for work.

Waiting for a cab, she told Ted about the phone call she received last night and he made a mental note to put a tap on her line. He also knew that Marcel would need to be notified that she was receiving more calls. Marcel would want Ted to make sure that she was safe and Ted also knew that Marcel would pay whatever it took to make that happen. As soon as Stasha was in the cab and on her way to work, Ted made the call. As he predicted, Marcel wanted all the bases covered. Ted had to have the line tap put on before she got home and Marcel wanted him to call him if anything else happened. Ted assured him that he would call him directly. Marcel sat in his office, but he wanted to be with his daughter. He wanted to make sure she was kept safe. The only thing that bothered Marcel was that they never knew when the bastard was going to strike again. This bastard, in Marcel's eyes, beat the hell out of his daughter, left her for dead, and then they heard nothing for almost three years. The police had no leads because of Stasha's memory loss. Marcel didn't care how much money he had to spend to keep his girl safe, but if he was to go to her for no reason, she was smart and would know that he had kept tabs on her all these years. He didn't know how she would respond to that. Years ago, he watched his wife slip away from him and he could do nothing. He had the power to protect his daughter, and he planned to use it. He only wished that, when they did catch the son of bitch, he would have five minutes with him alone. Just five minutes, Marcel thought.

CHAPTER 11

The days seemed to slip by for Stasha and Philip. The progress that was being made on the prototype was coming along better than they expected. Both of them had been working sixteen-hour days, and so much had happened in the month since she had gotten back from Montreal. Philip had been a regular at her apartment and, sometimes, she wondered if he would move in somewhere along the way. Stasha told him that Franny would be able to come with them when they went home for Canada Day and Philip informed her that Brad was going to fly in that day and he would be picking him up at the airport in the morning.

Philip told Stasha how Brad and he had been friends for years. Stasha couldn't wait for the day to be over so she could go home and pack. Philip had arranged for his plane to take them. A car would pick up Franny first, and then come to Stasha's to pick up Philip and her. Sitting at his desk, Philip rubbed the back of his neck and glanced at the clock. "I think it's time we pack it in. How about going to get something to eat and then head home?"

Stasha smiled at him and told him that she thought it was a great idea. She also thought about how Philip referred to her place as home and noticed that he packed his bags the night before and brought them over that morning.

Philip put all the documents in the safe and cleared off his desk. Walking up behind Stasha, he put his arms around her waist and nuzzled the back of her neck. If anyone would have told him a month ago that he would be head over heels in love with someone, he would have laughed at them. Now, he knew how it felt and he marveled at the thought that this beautiful woman in his arms was his. Letting her go, he walked over to get her coat and held it for her.

Stasha still couldn't believe that she had fallen in love so fast. She didn't want to tell him yet because some guys seemed to get spooked, and she was determined to let him be the first to say something. Stepping out onto the street, they decided to walk to their favorite restaurant. The same restaurant that Philip brought her to the first time they had lunch. Sitting at their regular booth, both ordered a soup, salad, and hot beef sandwich. They discussed when they would get together with both companies board of directors because they planned to have the project assembled and ready for production by the end of the summer.

"So how does it feel being a partner in one of the biggest firms in New York?" Philip asked her.

Stasha had still been in shock until they signed the papers a few days ago. "I still feel like it is a dream and that I will wake up and realize that it never happened. Tom plans to take his wife on a second honeymoon, but Ida tells me that she considers it a first because Tom was working so hard the first time that he spent most of the time on the phone." Stasha also told Philip how she sat with Tom and Ida at their house when she was signing the papers. "They had me in tears, Philip. This wonderful couple had told me that they had wanted this for a while, but didn't know how to ask me. Tom told me that the reason he pushed me so hard was to prepare me for this day. Sitting together and holding each others hand, they told me that I was like the child they never had."

Philip could see the tears starting to form in her eyes and knew that Tom and Ida had made the right choice. Stasha loved them just as much. "Did you tell your dad yet?" Philip asked her. He knew that Marcel was going to be so happy for her.

Looking at Philip, she told him, "No, I haven't told him yet. With everything going on and just signing the papers the other day, I thought that I would just wait till we got home to tell him."

Philip knew that it was killing her to hold in this kind of news, but he couldn't wait to see the look on Marcel's face when she told him. After finishing their supper, Philip paid the bill and they walked out to catch a cab. As the cab pulled over, Philip held the door to allow Stasha to get in.

On the way back to the apartment, Stasha leaned her head on Philip's shoulder and closed her eyes. It had been a tough week. All the emotions that she experienced this week were coming all at once. Stasha was glad that they decided to take a couple of extra days when they went home. Once Philip and Stasha arrived at her building, Philip had to wake Stasha up because she had fallen asleep on the way home. Opening the door, Philip let Stasha in and then took her coat and put both of them away. Stasha sat on the couch and put her feet up on the table. Philip went to the bar and poured a glass of wine for both of them and sat next to Stasha on the couch. Sitting back and sipping her wine, Stasha realized that she hadn't heard her messages on her machine. Reaching over, she pushed the button and the first message was from Franny. She was excited about going on Philip's plane and how Stasha knew how to pick them. At this, Stasha looked over at Philip and started to apologize to him for Franny's remark. Philip knew what she was going to do and told her not to worry about it. The next two messages where from Tara at the office.

The last message played out while Philip and Stasha sat comfortably and listened. "If you don't kill this project I will make sure that both the project and you never see the light of day."

As they listened, Philip jumped up and went over to the machine and pushed the button to replay the message. "Is this the first call that you've received here?" he asked her.

Stasha told him that she received one about two weeks ago, but couldn't hear the whole message. "I erased it because I couldn't hear the whole thing and put it from my mind," she told him.

Philip was getting very upset because now the son of a bitch was calling her at home. That meant that he knew where she lived. "Did you call the police about it?"

Stasha shook her head. She didn't make a big deal of it and was now scared that she didn't do so.

Philip told her that he would be back in a few minutes and walked out the door. Going down the elevator, he saw Ted standing near the entrance. "Hi Ted, I know that your working for Mr. Monteau and I have to ask you, did you know that Stasha received a threatening message on her machine today?"

Ted could see that Philip was going to be one person that wanted answers and Mr. Monteau had told him that Philip knew what was going on and to work with him. "I know that the call came in at two fifty-eight this afternoon. We had a trace put out on the call, but it came from a cell phone and we didn't have enough time to get the location pinpointed," Ted told Philip.

Philip walked away and ran his hand through his hair. Turning around, he looked at Ted and told him that he would do anything that was needed to catch the bastard. Philip handed Ted a card and told him that if extra men were needed that Ted would have authorization to call for them and that Philip would take care of the expense. "I know that you're doing the best you can, but I won't take any risk with this lady and I don't want you to have your guys overworked. If you need more, you call for it, ok?"

Ted thanked him and told him that everything was in place for their travel tomorrow and that Ted assigned a woman to stay in the apartment that was part of his team so that whoever this guy was would think she was still there instead of Montreal.

Philip agreed that it was a good plan. If the guy would make his move while they were gone, then Philip would be able to stop worrying about Stasha so much. Philip wished that the project was done and production was started on. The one thing that he kept thinking about was who would want this project killed? Second, who knew about the project? Going back upstairs, Philip made a mental note to have a buddy of his look into the situation. Ted seemed like a great guy, but Philip wasn't going to take any chances with Stasha. Opening the door, he looked over to the couch and saw that it didn't take her long to fall asleep. Walking over, he noticed, as he did many times before, that she was beautiful even in sleep. Picking her up, Stasha rested her head in the crook of his neck and wrapped her arms around it. Philip laid her gently on the bed. As she stirred from sleep, he told her that he was going to lock up.

Coming back into the room, Stasha lay under the covers on her side, and with sleepy eyes watched as Philip remove his clothes. As he removed his shirt, Stasha watched as his muscles rippled with each movement. She loved the way he looked. He wasn't built up like muscle builders, but a person could admire the definition that did show. She hated the look of large muscles, but Philip's were just right. Stasha's eyes were drawn to his hands and watched as he undid his pants and took them off. Philip was enjoying the fact that Stasha wasn't shy about him undressing in front of her. In fact, Philip guessed that, by the look on her face, she was enjoying herself, so he wanted to make sure she received a good show. As he climbed into bed beside her, he could see the desire in her eyes. Stasha's skin felt like velvet under his hands. His hand cupped her breast and his thumb lightly rubbed over her nipple until it came erect. Stasha could feel the sensation deep within her and felt it build.

As Philip took his time circling the one nipple, he lowered his head to the other breast and with his tongue began to lick it slowly. Stasha wanted the feeling to go on forever and put her hands in his hair to keep him there. Philip moved his hand down between them and stroked her belly as he traveled to the one place he needed to be. Stasha went regularly to have a Brazilian done and Philip was amazed to feel skin instead of hair in that moist region. At first, it took him off guard because he had never seen that before, but, since being with Stasha, he loved what she did for him. The sensation it caused for both of them was something he couldn't explain, but knew that now he would not have it any other way. Applying just a small amount of pressure against her clitoris, he waited just a few seconds before he inserted his finger. The sensation threw Stasha over the top and she came in Philip's hand.

As Stasha came back to earth, she rolled on top of Philip, and with small, slow kisses, descended down the length of his body. Philip was devoid of hair on his chest and Stasha loved having her lips on smooth skin. Making her way down, she stopped at his waist and looked up to see his eyes watching her, knowing that the feeling of passion was rising within him. Stasha knew what she was doing to him and felt the rush of excitement surge through her. Moving lower, she cupped his sac in her hand and massaged both testicles until she could feel them fill. Taking him into her mouth, she savored the taste of him. Being able to pleasure him this way was wonderful. Eric always liked to be the participant, but never gave back what was given.

Philip had to stop her before he came. He reached down and, in an instant, had her on her back and thrust himself to the hilt. Stasha never experienced lovemaking the way she did with Philip and knew that he would hold on until they could both climax together. Philip felt Stasha starting to climax and let himself go. Together, they both drifted into a place filled with wonder. Laying there spent, Philip finally gathered enough energy to move off Stasha and gathered her against him. Every time they made love, it always felt like the first time. Stasha was willing to try anything and Philip never disappointed her.

It had only been about six weeks since they had met and Philip was glad that his mother made the point that he was to attend the wedding with them. He thought about the first day seeing Stasha, and couldn't believe his luck that now he was laying beside her. Holding her close, he realized that she was asleep from her slow breathing. He was tired also, but the message kept playing back in his mind. Who else knew what they were working on? Why did they want something that could save millions of lives be destroyed? Pulling Stasha closer to him, he drifted off to sleep, making a promise to keep her safe. He was glad that they would be getting out of New York for a while. It could give his friend time to look into a few things that Philip wanted checked out.

The next morning, Stasha stretched and felt wonderful. Lying in bed, she could hear the shower running and knew that Philip would be ready to go soon. Getting up, she made the bed and straightened the room up. Going to the closet, she took out a pair of jeans and a soft pink shirt. Putting them on the bed, she walked to the bathroom and opened the door to find that Philip just finished. "I guess I'm too late to join you." Stasha laughed.

"I could get back in, but then I wouldn't have breakfast ready when you came out," Philip told her and smiled as he walked by and smacked the bottom she so proudly displayed.

Stasha could hear him laughing as she turned on the water. Standing there, she let the hot water rinse away the tiredness that had been holding on for the last few days. Washing her hair and then her body, she reflected on everything that had happened. She knew from the reaction Philip showed her last night that the message was more serious that she had imagined. She just thought it was one of those prank calls that people get and didn't want anyone to think she was afraid and needed help. Philip showed her that it wasn't just a prank. She would talk to him and find out what he knew. After toweling off and getting dressed, Stasha blow dried her hair and put it up in a clip. Sitting down at her vanity, she applied her make-up. Finishing up and putting what make-up she was going to bring with her into her suitcase, she went to the kitchen to have breakfast. Going to the counter and grabbing the coffee pot, she poured herself a cup of coffee. Stasha took a seat at the table and Philip put her plate in front of her.

Two hard boiled eggs and a slice of ham, sliced tomatoes, whole wheat toast, and sliced oranges were neatly arrange on the plate. The man loved to cook and Stasha was willing to do anything to make him happy. They had the arrangement that if Philip cooked, Stasha cleaned up after. She thought that it was the best arrangement. She loved to cook too, but would allow Philip free use of her kitchen anytime.

"Philip, why did you get so upset last night after hearing the message on my machine? Is there something that I should know about?"

Philip thought about it last night and knew that, to protect her, she needed to protect herself. She needed to know everything that had been happening, but he also knew that he was not the person to tell her. She needed to hear from Marcel all the things he had done to keep her safe all these years. Philip would talk to Marcel when they went to Montreal. "I don't like the fact that some weirdo has your phone number."

Stasha thought that it was sweet that he was worried about her, but she had lived in New York for quite a few years and had been able to take care of herself all that time. Stasha decided not to say anything. When a man wants to protect his woman, Stasha thought, let him because they never listen to you concerning those types of matters anyway. Cleaning up the dishes while Philip finished getting dress, Stasha was getting excited about going home for Canada Day. Her father always had a big party. The nice thing about it was that it was casual. Jeans or shorts were ok. Stasha had called Marcel yesterday at lunch and he was just as excited as she was. They talked about the restaurant and Marcel told her that she needed to sign some papers when she got home. He would go through everything with her.

Philip walked into the living room with their luggage and called down to see if their car was there. "Are you ready, Stasha? I have all your bags here and your coat. The car is downstairs waiting."

Stasha checked everything one more time and knew Mary would be in so she wasn't worried. Putting her beige jacket over her arm, she followed Philip out the door and turned to make sure that it was locked. Franny had called the night before and asked if they could pick her up on the way to the airport. She had a bit more packing to do. Philip told Stasha that it would be fine.

As they headed over to Franny's place to pick her up, Stasha turned to him, "Philip, I know that this is the first time that you are actually meeting Franny. I need you to know that she is like my sister. I will never give up my friendship with her. I really hope that you like her because it would be so much easier."

Philip looked at her and asked, "Where did that come from? Sweetheart, any friend of yours I know I will like. You have a great perception of people and I can't see you being friends with a mean person."

Stasha was holding her breath while she listened to Philip and finally let it out. Franny was very important to her and she was so relieved that Philip was going to wait before he passed judgment. She didn't want to lose Philip, but Eric gave her a choice and he was the one who lost. She hoped that Philip never gave her the same choice.

Pulling up to Franny's apartment, Stasha jumped out and ran up to Franny who was so excited that she was waiting outside with her luggage. Both girls embraced and laughed at being so excited to go home for the holiday.

Philip watched all this while leaning against the car. After hugging Stasha, Franny looked at the man waiting by the car.

Turning back to Stasha, Franny asked "Is this the man that you have been hiding from me?" Franny smiled at Stasha when she saw her friend nod. Franny could tell just by looking at her that this man was making her happy. She never liked Eric. She saw how he would treat her best friend and told him on a number of occasions. Franny promised to wait and see how this one turned out.

Philip came over to the two women who still stood on the sidewalk and mentioned that the driver had Franny's bags in the car and if they were to get to the airport they would need to leave. He escorted them to the car and let Franny sit beside Stasha and took the other seat that faced them. On their way to the airport, Philip wanted to get to know Franny better since she was so close to the woman that he loved. "Franny, Stasha has told me that you're a nurse at Mount Sinai Hospital."

Franny was still in awe with everything happening around her, but was happy that Philip was interested in what she did. "Yes, when Stasha decided to move out to New York, I couldn't let her come alone. Being a nurse in the OR, jobs are needed all around the world. Getting a job at Mount Sinai was just a bonus." Franny remembered the uncertainty that she felt when going into the interview all those years ago. Walking out with the job had been one of her proudest moments.

All three talked on the way to the airport and were in such deep conversation about the holidays that they didn't realize that they were already there. Philip escorted the women to the plane. Once they were settled and in the air, Philip asked if Franny would like something to drink as he poured a glass of juice for Stasha.

"I would love a glass of water if you wouldn't mind."

Philip took another glass out and added juice to it. Grabbing a bottle of water out of the fridge, he brought all the drinks over to them and sat down to relax for the rest of the trip. Stasha could see that Franny had a number of questions to ask her and knew that the two of them would have a nice chat when they got home. Philip liked Franny; she was a down to earth person. He could understand why Stasha and she maintained their friendship for so long. Franny filled Philip in on the funny stories that both Stasha and Franny went through as children and added a few of his own. The time flying home was filled with laughter to the point that on a few occasions it had them in tears.

Philip didn't tell Stasha, but he wanted to meet Franny first before introducing her to Brad when he arrived in Montreal. Brad had been so serious lately that Franny was just what he needed to bring the life back into him. Philip had hoped that Brad would take the time off to come for the holiday and was glad when Brad informed him that he could make it. When they landed in Montreal, Philip had a car ready for them. Once Philip had the ladies seated safely in the back of the car, he joined them after noticing that one of the men he hired had given him the nod that everything was clear. Philip didn't want to take the chance that the sicko that had probably been the same person to beat Stasha half to death, follow them. He wasn't going to give him the chance to hurt her again. Once he had the chance to sit down with Marcel to talk about the problem that needed to be taken care of, the better he would feel. In the meantime, he wanted to enjoy the holiday just as much as the rest of them. Working on the project and worrying about Stasha left him emotionally drained.

CHAPTER 12

Dropping Franny off at her parents, Philip put his arms around Stasha and the both of them just enjoyed the moment. Knowing that the next few days were going to be hectic, they took a few moments for themselves. Arriving at Stasha's house, Philip helped her with the luggage and went into the house.

Marcel was in the den when they arrived. Turning to see his daughter, he got up from his chair and went over to giver her a hug. After shaking hands with Philip, they all settled into the chairs and Marcel poured them all a drink.

Monique came through the doors and smiled at them all. "I thought I heard the car pull up," she said. As she walked over to Stasha, she could tell that she was worn out. Turning to Philip, she asked, "Philip, would you like to join us for supper?"

Philip always liked Monique. She was always kind to his family. "No, I'm sorry, but I must decline this time, even though the aroma that I smell is delicious. Mother would hang me from the rafters if I did not spend the evening with them. I know that Stasha could use some rest. Next time, I promise to stay." Getting up, he looked at Marcel. The look that passed between the both of them told Marcel that some things needed to be attended to, but would hold for the next day.

Marcel nodded in understanding and shook Philip's hand. Stasha walked Philip to the door and put her arms around his neck. "It is going to feel funny without you beside me tonight," she told him with a smile.

Philip kissed her and told her to get some rest and that he would call her tomorrow. After seeing him drive away, Stasha closed the door and walked back to the den. Curling up in the chair, she picked up her glass of wine and took a sip. "Where did Dad go?" she asked Monique.

"He just took your bags upstairs and will be back down. You look so tired, Stasha. Are you taking care of yourself?"

Stasha could see the concern in Monique's eyes and reassured her that everything was fine. She told Monique about the progress that they were making and how, after the holidays, they would be able to put the prototype together. "Things are moving a lot faster than we thought and I really can't believe that we will have it finished so soon." When Stasha thought about the project in the beginning, it was a hopeful dream that she promised herself would come true. Now, that day was so close. Marcel came back into the room and watched the two ladies that he loved the most in this world getting along so well.

Monique noticed Marcel and knew that he would want some time with Stasha, so she got up and told them both that supper would be ready soon and that Stasha would have time to lay down for an hour or so. Marcel was glad that Monique gave them time to spend together, but also caught the hint from his wife. He thought his wife was a smart woman, but now knew that she was a good director of things that would have escaped his vision. Marcel didn't want to keep her any longer than possible, but wanted to find out how she was and if she would share anything with him.

Stasha didn't realize until now that she was tired, but she also wanted to spend time with her dad. They talked about the project, and then she told him about the phone calls. "Dad I know that voice, but I can't remember where I heard it. It seems to be on the tip of my memory, but as much as I try, it just won't come forward."

Marcel reminded her that the doctors told her that her memory would come back eventually. Seeing that her eyes were trying to stay open, he suggested that she go upstairs and freshen up and have a nap and they would wake her when supper was ready. Stasha didn't need to be told twice. She kissed her father and went upstairs to her room. Going into the bathroom, Stasha turned on the hot water and went to remove her clothes. After undressing, she went to the tub and turned off the water. Stepping into the tub and sitting down, she let the hot water seep into her bones. Once the water cooled, Stasha stepped out and dried off. Putting on a big T-shirt, she climbed into bed and was asleep before her head hit the pillow.

Stasha heard the knock on her door and Monique popped her head in. " I didn't want to wake you dear, but we are going to eat in half an hour and I wanted you to have some time to get ready." Stasha thanked her and looked at the clock. It was four thirty, and she realized she slept for almost two hours. Stretching, she got out of bed and went to her luggage. Pulling out a blouse and some jeans she went over to the bed and sat down. Taking off her T-shirt, she grabbed her blouse and put it on. After slipping on her jeans, she walked into the bathroom and brushed her hair and put on a little mascara and lipstick. After making the bed, she went downstairs.

Monique had roast beef, mashed potatoes, and baby carrots all ready for them, and some fresh buns with creamy butter. As they sat around the table eating, Monique and Marcel told Stasha of the plans for the Canada Day celebration. Marcel told her how Monique and Marcel had sat down with Armand and Jose, Philip's parents, and Evette and Ben, Franny's parents, and talked about having one party instead of three. All of them thought that, since their children all came home together, it would be a great idea. They all chipped in and found out that they were going to have a grand party and the expense was actually cheaper for all. Plus, since all three parents had been friends for years, it only made sense to enjoy the day together. They had rented a pavilion at Park De La Riviere Des Mille-Lies and there would be lots of food and drink for everyone. Fireworks were planned for the evening and they even hired a bus for people who drank throughout the day. Marcel only hoped that it would be a nice day for the activities. Stasha knew that it was going to be a party that would be talked about for a while. It would also save Stasha, Philip, and Franny time from jumping from one party to the next.

Stasha thanked Monique for the great supper and got up to help with the dishes. Marcel went into the den to make a few phone calls and the women stayed in the kitchen to have some coffee and talk about the rest of the family. She told her how Annette and Michael would not be able to make it because it was a busy time for Michael in Niagara Falls. Being a tourist attraction, he and the family would attend the big celebration in Niagara Falls for Canada Day. Mathew would be coming tomorrow with Joan and Andre and their new baby girl they named Michelle. Jacqueline would be here. Alex and Melanie would be coming in tomorrow.

Stasha was disappointed that Annette and Michael would not be coming, but understood what work could do to you and the responsibilities that went along with it. It seemed like everything was taken care of and Stasha knew everyone was going to have a great time. The phone rang and Monique answered it. Nodding her head towards Stasha, she told her it was Franny. Stasha went to take the phone from Monique and sat down in the nearest chair. Franny could talk someone's ear off if given the chance and Stasha knew that she better get comfortable.

"Stasha, Mom and Dad just told me about the plans for the party. Isn't it great? Now we can all celebrate together. You have a great Dad. I know that Philip's parents are well off and your dad is too, but they never made my parents seem beneath them. My mom was telling me that all six of them sat down and made sure that the party could be paid equally without added cost and show. How we are going to have a potluck instead of having it catered and everyone is to bring drinks that can be shared by all." Franny loved Stasha's dad because, even though Franny didn't have a nice house like them or anything expensive like they did growing up, he always treated Franny the same as he treated Stasha. Growing up, Stasha and Franny got grounded by both parents, and Marcel, Ben, and Evette always carried through with the other parent's rules. "I know that Mom and Dad don't make much money, but to have people like the LaRoch treat my parents the way your dad does brings tears to my eyes."

Stasha did have tears in her eyes at this point. She had met Philip's parents at the wedding briefly with his sister Lizabeth and wasn't given too much time to speak to them. Stasha knew that her father felt a kinship with Ben and Evette because of the hard times that they helped Marcel through, not only when his wife died, but with Evette helping him with raising a girl. Marcel would be the first person to stand behind Ben if the need came. The only thing that bothered Stasha was that, even though Ben didn't have a big company like her father or *Monsieur* LaRoch, Franny forgets that her father was the most wanted carpenter in Canada. He made good money, but Franny could never forget the time when he didn't. Stasha knew that Franny would never get past that time, but Stasha would never talk about this subject because it wasn't worth the fight that Franny would start. When they were teenagers and Franny's dad was making good money with all the contracts he was receiving, Franny was talking to Stasha about how she would finally be in the same league as her. Stasha told her that they had never been on different levels, but Franny wouldn't listen.

When Stasha went home in tears and told her father what had happened, Marcel asked Ben and Evette to bring Franny over. As they sat in the den, Marcel told Ben and Evette what had transpired between the girls. Marcel saw the look of sadness cross Ben's face and Marcel told Franny that he never looked down on her parents and that he felt they were part of his family. That Ben was more like a brother to him and Evette like a sister. Franny was in tears as Marcel spoke. Marcel shook hands with Ben, and Ben and Evette apologized for Franny's attitude. Ben and Evette reassured Marcel that they felt the same as he did and did not know where the notion came to their daughter that it was anything different. Marcel went over to Franny, who was sobbing so hard that she sometimes missed a breath, and he gathered her in his arms. "'*Ma petite*' never think that I would think less of you or your family. People do not judge by the wallet, but by the heart. I think of you as a daughter. Now you must stop this crying because I know that you feel sorry for saying that."

Franny hugged Marcel and through her tears told him that she did and she would never think that way again. Turning to Stasha, Franny ran over to her and hugged her and told her how sorry she was. She asked Stasha if she could ever forgive her.

Now, sitting on the phone and listening to Franny talk, Stasha knew that sometimes Franny referred to the subject, but Stasha knew that she did it unintentionally. "So, are Andre, Tina, and Jean-Paul and the family coming?" Stasha asked. It had been a long time since she had seen them all. Stasha remembered being a part of the family and playing with Tina and Andre. Jean-Paul always seem to lord over them and, being the oldest, took the most of the wrath from his parents. Sometimes, Stasha remembered when she had gotten hurt or suddenly didn't feel well; Jean-Paul was nice to her. Even growing up, Stasha thought he was the nicest looking guy in Montreal, but he always looked at her as a sister and, not to mention, she was eight years younger than him, but it didn't stop her from dreaming.

"Yes, Mom said that everyone took the time off. They were only unsure that I would make it. You have to admit, I haven't been home to often with all the overtime at the hospital. Well I guess it's time to go. With everything happening today and visiting with everyone I'm completely drained. I'll call you tomorrow."

Stasha said good bye and hung up the phone. Stasha pushed the chair back to the table and went to the living room to watch some television. Both Monique and Marcel were sitting on the couch watching an action movie. Marcel loved action movies. Stasha preferred the comedy movies because she loved to laugh. Walking over to the bar, she poured herself a glass of wine and curled up in the overstuffed chair by the couch. She realized that the three of them had never shared a night like this before, just sitting here watching a movie like a normal family. Stasha knew that if she hadn't been so stubborn for so long that they probably could have shared a lot more nights like this.

The movie was good. It showed the courage of one man who saved his buddies out of the enemy-infested jungle and, even though he was a hero, didn't take recognition for the acts that he did. In the end, Stasha and Monique had tears in their eyes. Getting up, Stasha wished them both good night and went upstairs to her room. Opening the door, Stasha was still amazed that her room was the same as when she was a girl. She really wanted to tell Monique that she could redo the room in any way that she wanted. Little girls had to grow up eventually. Slipping into her T-shirt, because, even though her dad had the air conditioning on, it was still humid. He didn't like it to get to cool in the house. Lying on top of the covers, Stasha tried to think about the voice on the message. She thought that if she just laid here and didn't try to force it, the memory would come. Closing her eyes, she focused on the voice. In the next instant, she was running down the hallway and could hear someone, but couldn't figure out where he was. Panic was setting in and she knew that she had to get help. She could see the elevator ahead. Running towards it, she thought, just a few more steps and she'd be safe. Just as she reached the elevator, strong arms came around her neck and started to squeeze. "Help me! Help me!" she could hear herself scream, but because of the arms around her neck, the shouts for help only came out as a whisper.

Stasha woke, a cold sweat having made a film all over her. She was soaked with it. Getting up, she walked into the bathroom and turned on the hot water. She felt so cold. Standing under the hot shower, she let it seep into her muscles that she just realized were strung so tight she thought they would rip. This was the first time that she had seen an elevator in the dream. She also knew that she was running from someone and was trying to get out. After stepping out of the shower, Stasha dried herself off and picked out another oversized T-shirt from her luggage. Crawling into bed, she thought about how close she must be coming to the truth of what happened that night. She thought about telling her dad or Philip, but decided that the only thing she had seen was the elevator, so it wasn't much to go on. Turning out the light, Stasha rolled on her side and drifted of to sleep.

CHAPTER 13

Canada Day started in a whirlwind. There was so much still to do and they were packing up the van with food. Philip called earlier that morning to tell Stasha that he had to pick up Brad at the airport and would meet her at the park. Stasha thought that it was a good plan. She wouldn't have had any time to give him anyway with trying to get everything packed and having her shower. It was supposed to be a hot day, so Stasha opted for some white shorts and a pink tank top. She put her hair in two braids and wore only the necessary make-up, mascara, and lipstick. She had started tanning back home and had a good base, but brought along her sunscreen anyway. She tried to protect her skin as much as possible.

Marcel put the last of the boxes of food in the van and went to get Monique. Coming out of the house, Monique was all smiles. Wearing a pale yellow sundress and a straw hat with the same color ribbon that matched the dress and white flat sandals, she was ready to go. Marcel locked up and got into the van, then drove them to the park. Finding a parking place close to their pavilion, Marcel parked the van and Stasha got out and looked over to where all the people were celebrating.

She didn't think that there were going to be so many people, but her father always said the more the merrier. Going to the back of the van, Stasha started to help bring the boxes over to where the others had already started setting up the food. Armand and Ben were standing by the barbeque that Ben had brought for the occasion. Evette and Jose were instructing the girls on where to place everything under the pavilion. There were many tables set up so people would have a place to sit while eating. Children were running around and the smaller ones were trying to keep up. Stasha could hear laughter coming from all directions. This is going to be a good day, she thought to herself. Putting the one box she carried on the ground next to the table, she turned to go and get the others and noticed that it was already being taken care of by some of the men there. Turning back to the box she brought, she started placing items on the table where the older women told her. Reaching down to get the last item, she felt strong arms come around her waist and tensed for just a second.

Philip nuzzled her ear and brought her closer to him. "Well, I have never seen white shorts worn so well and these legs seem to go on forever."

"Well, hello to you, too," Stasha said as she turned around and put her arms around his neck. Philip leaned down and gave those inviting lips a kiss, not caring who saw them. The last few months had been great and he didn't want to push her into anything she wasn't ready for. As they finished the kiss, Stasha noticed a few eyes on them and smiled. Brad was walking towards them and, besides Philip; she would have said he was the most gorgeous man she had ever seen. He was tall and was in great physical shape. Brad's hair was black as a raven's and the tan he had made Stasha envious. Philip turned around to see what caught her attention and saw Brad coming towards them. Putting his arm around her waist, Philip gestured for Brad to come over.

"You remember Brad, Stasha?" Philip asked. As Brad extended his hand to shake Stasha's, he noticed a firm grip and was surprised and pleased. Brad also noticed how incredibly beautiful this woman was that his best buddy had attached himself to.

"Miss Monteau, it is nice to see you again." Brad thought that Philip was one lucky son of a bitch to be able to find a woman who not only looked like this, but had brains too. Brad knew that Stasha was the one who brought the project up to the forefront and invented the concept.

"Brad, please call me Stasha if we are going to be friends," Stasha told him.

Turning to Philip, Brad smiled and said, "So, if you picked the rose from this city does that mean you left thorns for the rest of us?" he said laughing. Stasha knew of one rose that was still in the garden, but wanted to talk just a little bit more to Brad before introducing them. Franny wouldn't be here for another hour. Evette said that she had a restless night and gave her time to sleep in. Ben would be going to get her soon.

The three of them grabbed a drink off the beverage table. They spotted a table under some trees and thought they better grab it before they had to take one in the sun. Sitting down, Stasha asked Brad a bit about himself and Brad knew that Stasha would like to know what kind of person Philip hung out with and didn't mind answering the questions. He, in turn, asked some questions himself and was happy to find out that she was financially independent and didn't have to worry about Philip being taken for a ride in the future. As they sat there talking, Brad filled Stasha in on the crazy stunts they both did in university. Stasha never laughed as hard as she did listening to the stories Brad told her.

Philip tried to tell her that Brad was the instigator of most of them, but she knew that the both of them had conspired together in the stunts. As Brad was in the middle of the next story, he stopped talking and was looking behind Stasha. Both Philip and Stasha turned to see Franny coming over to join them. As she reached the table, Brad's jaw dropped. He loved all kinds of women, but the small, petite ones always did something to him.

"Hey, Stasha, Mom told me that you were entertaining some very attractive men over here and I was to get my butt over here to help you out."

Stasha laughed and introduced her to Brad. Philip was kind to both of them when he informed Franny that Brad was also single. Brad knew that he could count on Philip to open the way for him. Brad also knew that Stasha's friend came on the plane with them, which would have given Philip time to find out something about her. Philip wouldn't have introduced him that way if he didn't think that she was ok.

Franny sat down next to Stasha, and Philip went to sit on the other side with Brad. Philip asked Stasha if she would like a refill of her drink and Brad noticing that Franny didn't have one and offered to get her something. Both women thanked them, and as the men went to the beverage table, Franny wasted no time getting the goods on Brad.

"So, how come you didn't tell me that Philip had such a gorgeous friend who happened to be single?"

Stasha had a smile on her face because she knew that that would be the first question Franny would ask. "This is only the second time I've met him, and the first time was only for few minutes. Philip told me that Brad would be coming for the celebration. He does seem like a nice guy and Philip would not have him as his lawyer if he wasn't trustworthy."

Franny perked up at the word lawyer. A lot of guys she met lately had ok jobs, but she didn't want to be the main supporter of the family if it ever came to be. She had worked hard to get where she was and wanted to find someone who did the same.

Brad took the time to find out what he could about Franny. Philip told him that she was a nurse at Mount Sinai hospital and that he had just met her on the plane coming here. Stasha told him that she was single and worked a lot of hours at the hospital because there was a shortage of nurse right now. Brad was happy that he could make it for this getaway, but things were looking better and better.

As the guys came back with drinks, Franny couldn't get over how green Brad's eyes were; the thick dark lashes made them appealing. As they talked, time flew by. Lunch was being put out and all four decided to eat, and then get on one of the teams for baseball that would start afterwards. Brad and Philip walked over with Franny and Stasha to the buffet that was set out.

Ben was at the grill and noticed the tall man with his daughter. Armand had been telling him about Brad and Ben could see from his daughter's face that she was interested in the man standing beside her. He was not the type of father to interfere, but Franny was special to him and he didn't want her to get hurt. Armand had reassured him that she was in good hands.

Franny had to smile at Brad because Philip had just told her how Brad loved food and, by the way his plate was heaped, she knew that Philip spoke the truth. The four of them talked some more while they ate and Brad was impressed at how intelligent Franny was. Often, when he had met women, they only saw looks and the job. Franny asked him questions about his work and listened to the answers. He, in return, had asked her about her work and didn't realize how hard it was. Dealing with death and seeing people in different stages of illness had to be hard on anyone.

After they finished lunch, they walked over to the baseball diamond to play ball. Their team lost by two runs, but everyone had a great time. Philip suggested a walk by the river and Brad and the girls thought it would be a great idea. Franny and Brad walked ahead of them and Stasha thought how nice it was that Franny and Brad seemed to click right off. Walking hand in hand with Philip was so relaxing. They didn't talk, but just enjoyed the scenery around them and each other.

Philip laughed and asked Stasha if she had seen Brad's face when Franny took off her sunglasses to play baseball. "I thought he was going to fall because I never seen him do a double take so fast in my life." Stasha laughed too. She knew that Franny had the most beautiful eyes and most men stopped in their tracks when she pointed them their way. They were very exotic and the blue was a color so deep that when men looked into them, most were lost.

Franny saw the reaction she got from Brad and she was pleased with the effect she was having on him. This was one man that she would like to see more of. When they came back from the river, the girls went over to help with the supper preparations and the men went over to stand with Marcel, Ben, and Armand. Armand introduced Philip and Brad to Ben. Ben listened to the two men as they talked to Armand and Marcel. Marcel took Philip aside and asked Philip if there was anything new about the guy they were looking for.

"No, sir, but Marcel, I don't like the fact that she is receiving calls at home. This guy knows where she lives and that worries me more than I like to admit."

Marcel told him that he was working on an angle that might give him a clue as to who this person might be. They both agreed that when Philip got back to New York they would see about bringing this guy out in the open. Time was of the essence now that the prototype would be completed and then sent off for government approval. If this guy wanted the project killed before that step, both men didn't want Stasha to run into the same fate that happened three years earlier.

Stasha and Franny went over to Philip and Brad. Stasha handed each of them a beer, and then took her glass of wine from Franny. Stasha had seen Marcel and Philip in deep discussion as she was walking over and when they saw her coming they dropped the subject.

As Philip put his arm around her, she asked her father, "So what had you two so deep in conversation?"

Philip looked at Marcel, and then looked down at Stasha and smiled, "I was just telling your dad that I just may steal you away, and he was informing me that he wouldn't mind if I did." Stasha laughed and leaned her head against Philip. Franny noticed that her father was talking to Brad and was trying to get his attention to get him to stop. Brad saw Franny out of the corner of his eye and thought it comical how her dad knew what she was trying to do, but just ignored her. Brad didn't mind answering his questions. He would be protective too if he had a daughter that looked like her. Brad knew firsthand that there were a lot of creeps on the streets.

Everyone went to get something to eat, and then after supper the music was turned up so whoever wanted to dance until they started the fireworks were able to do so. Ben had brought a portable dance floor and most of the people there took advantage of it. Philip held Stasha in his arms as a slow tune came on the portable stereo someone brought. He loved the feel of her in his arms. Brad wasn't going to let an opportunity like this slip by and was happy when he asked Franny to dance and she accepted.

Both couples decided to go set up their blankets on the bank of the river. The fireworks would be starting soon. All four of them grabbed a drink and made their way to a perfect spot. Philip sat with Stasha sitting inside his legs and Franny just took it upon herself to do the same with Brad. Both girls sat leaning back against the men and enjoyed their wine and the show. As everyone packed up at the end of the evening, Philip told Stasha that he would call her tomorrow and

Brad asked Franny if she wouldn't mind if he called her also. Franny gave him her number and thanked him for a great time. As they left, Franny and Stasha went back to packing the rest of their stuff and loaded it into the van. It had been a successful celebration all around. Stasha was happy for Franny too. Brad seemed like a nice guy.

CHAPTER 14

The weekend flew by and Stasha waited for Philip to pick her up. All four of them would be going back to New York together. Brad and Franny had time to get to know each other over the weekend. Between Philip's family and her own, they always seemed to be on the go. Marcel came up to Stasha, who stood out front with her bags.

"I'm so glad that you had the chance to come home for the weekend. Philip is a good man. Are you happy?"

Stasha looked at her father and told him, "Yes, dad, I'm very happy. Philip is great and I'm glad that we get along so well. I want to take it slow with him though. You know what happened with Eric. I just don't want it to end up like that again."

Marcel would never forget what that man did to her. Marcel knew that if he had tried to tell her how he felt about Eric, she would never have listened. She had to find out about him on her own. The car pulled up and the driver came over to gather up her bags and put them in the trunk. Philip got out and shook Marcel's hand. "Well, have a good trip. Call me when you get home," Marcel told his daughter as he kissed her on the cheek.

Stasha couldn't wait to get back home. The prototype was to be completed this week, and then the information and testing was going to be sent to get the required testing that was needed from the government. Once it was sent off, it could take up to five years to get approved. The main thing was that they were actually in the process of sending it out. With Philip's knowledge, the project was that much closer. They made a good team and she looked forward to working with him on more projects in the future. Everyone was happy when they landed in New York.

Brad asked Franny if she needed a ride, which she accepted. Stasha relaxed against Philip on the way home. Once they reached her apartment, Philip grabbed their bags and brought them up. Opening the door, Stasha was taken back at what awaited her inside. The whole apartment was turned upside down. Philip looked around. No one was there. He told Stasha not to touch anything and used his cell phone to call Ted.

"Where is the person who was supposed to stay here?"

Ted told him that something came up and she wasn't able to stay last night. Ted told Philip that the only people that came through the front door had their names on a list. He told him that he would look into everyone that had access to the building. Somehow, the jerk got in.

There was no way that Philip was going to let Stasha stay here now. "Honey, I'm going to call the police. Without touching anything, can you see if anything was taken?" Stasha nodded and went around the apartment to see if anything was taken. She came back and waited for Philip to finish with the police. "They are sending someone over right now. Did you notice if anything is gone?"

Stasha couldn't believe that this had happened. "I talked to Mary and she said that everything was in order yesterday when she came in to clean. It must have happened sometime last night or early today."

Philip looked around. Who ever came in must have been looking for information on the project. Nothing was gone because Stasha had brought all the information about the device to his office once they started on it. Dialing his phone, he waited for it to be answered.

"Mr. Arnold, its Philip. How are things going at the lab?" Philip wanted to know if any occurrences happened. If not, then this guy didn't know that everything was kept there. He didn't know the connection between Stasha and him. With the merge of both companies and what had happened in the past, both Tom and himself thought it would be better not to make it public knowledge of the merge until they could get the prototype off.

"Everything is fine here. Things are going according to plan. Will you be in tomorrow?"

Philip was satisfied that everything was going well. He had the highest technology in security at the lab. "We've had an incident at

Stasha's. Someone went through everything looking for something. Make sure you do a double check of the security for safety's sake when you lock up. Yes, I will be in tomorrow. But if not, you can reach me at my place." Philip said good bye and put his phone back in his pocket.

The police showed up about fifteen minutes later and asked both of them questions. They looked around and asked Stasha if she had a place to stay while they had their investigators go through the place. Ted had informed them downstairs of the situation and they wanted to see if the guy left any prints behind.

"She will be staying with me for as long as it takes." Philip handed the officer his card and told him that if anything came up that he would appreciate a call. Philip had called for his driver to come and get them. When he arrived, Philip grabbed their bags and brought them down. Once they arrived at his place, they rode the elevator up. Opening the door, Stasha walked in and was astonished at how big his place was. It was her first time here because Philip always came over to her place. She had been content to have him at her place.

It was beautiful. She knew that he must have had an interior designer come in. It was very contemporary and masculine. Philip stood back and watched her reaction to his home. Turning around, Stasha told him, "This place is so beautiful. Its large enough to fit a huge family in."

Philip smiled because he sometimes thought the same thing. "I'm going to take the bags upstairs to the bedroom. Why don't you get us a drink? I'll be down in a minute. "

Stasha was still amazed at the size of his place and walked over to the bar and took a beer out of the fridge and poured herself a glass of wine. Noticing the wall to wall window, Stasha went to look at the view. It was spectacular. A person could see for miles up here. Turning, she walked over to the couch and sat down.

Philip came down and grabbed his beer off the bar and went to sit next to her. "We need to do some brainstorming, Stasha. This guy knows about the project, but how? Also, I would like to know if he is connected to the situation three years ago. Can you remember anything, anything at all of that night?"

Stasha tried to remember, but it just wouldn't come. She told him about the latest dream she had. She knew she was getting closer to remembering what happened, but the more she forced herself, the more frustrated she got.

Philip was more worried than ever now. The hit on Stasha's place was not only someone looking for something, but was also letting them know that he could get to her. She was safe now. To get up here, one needed a special card to arrive at the apartment. The guy would have to know some high tech people before he could have a card made. In the meantime, Philip was going to double his efforts to catch him before he did get close to her again. Sitting on the couch together seemed so right that Philip didn't want to move, but he knew that Stasha would be exhausted from traveling home, then with the incident at the apartment. "I'm going to go and have a shower, and then I will get the Jacuzzi ready for you. A long soak in it will loosen up those tense muscles and give you a good night sleep."

"Ok, I'm just going to call Franny to tell her where I'll be staying. If you don't mind, I want to give her your number. If she can't reach me at home, she will panic."

Philip thought it would be a good idea also and went upstairs to have the shower he needed. Plus, while Stasha soaked in the Jacuzzi, he would have a chance to talk to Marcel.

Stasha reached for the phone and dialed Franny's number. After two rings, Franny answered with her usual happy hello. "Hi Stasha, I just want to thank you for introducing me to Brad. He is such a great guy. When he drove me home, he was so polite and didn't even try those stupid lines that most guys use. Then, when we arrived here, he helped bring my bags up. He gave me his number and told me that he would like to hear from me this week so we could have dinner. Ah, I think its love."

Stasha was smiling while Franny went on and on about Brad. She really did deserve someone nice for a change. "Franny, I just wanted to tell you that I will be staying with Philip for a while. Once we got back to my place, we discovered that it had been broken into. Philip thinks that it is connected to what happened three years ago. I'm starting to believe that he may be right." Stasha told her how much damage was done, but nothing had been taken.

"Well I'm glad that you were with Philip when you walked in. I don't even want to fathom the thought if you went in by yourself and the creep was still there," she said. Franny was worried for her best friend now because she still remembered the night she was on at work when they brought her into the hospital all beaten up. They called her up in OR because some of the girls in emergency knew that Stasha was like a sister to her. When Franny ran down to the emergency room and saw her, she was in shock. She wanted to help work on her, but the attending doctor told her that she couldn't because of the closeness of their relationship. The only thing Franny could do at the time was to stand back and let them do their best to save her and pray.

"Let me give you Philip's number so you can get in touch with me. I don't know how long I will be staying here, but I won't be able to go back to my apartment until they finish gathering any evidence from that mess. Oh, Franny, when I walked into my bedroom, that creep had his hands all over my underwear. They were thrown everywhere. It felt like he touched me. That will be the first thing that I throw away."

Franny told her that when she finds out when her next day off would be, both of them would do a little shopping and look for things that needed to be replaced.

"That sounds like a great idea. I better let you go, I can hear that Philip is done with the shower and will be down shortly." After saying goodbye, Stasha sat back and took a sip of her wine.

Franny still had a hard time with what happened and Stasha always made sure that she knew how to get in touch with her after that. Philip came down a few minutes later with a pair of sweat pants that hung low on his hips. His chest was bare and his hair still wet and ruffled by the towel he was holding in his hand. Stasha thought to herself, *Wow, is he really mine?* Any woman would love to sit back and take in this picture and would probably go to bed with it still on her mind.

He looked up and caught the expression on her face and smiled. "I have it all set for you upstairs. Why don't you take your wine up with you and I'll come up in a bit." He wanted to speak with Marcel. What he had to say, he didn't want her hearing. She had enough to worry about right now.

Stasha got up and walked over to him and gave him a lingering kiss, and then went upstairs to enjoy the bath he'd prepared. Stasha was surprised when she walked into the bedroom. It had to be twice the size of hers. The furniture was a dark walnut and the floors were mahogany. The walls were a medium taupe color, which brought out the beauty in the wood, and on the floor was a large oriental carpet in different browns. Stasha undressed and put her clothes on the chair by the armoire and went into the bathroom. She stood in the doorway and took it all in. The bathroom was equally large and finished in a beige Italian marble. The vanity was to the left and took up the whole wall, and the sinks of glass sat on top of the marble counter. She remembered seeing that design in magazines, but never knew anyone who had them. To the right side was a shower that had so many jets in it that she thought to herself, someone could get blasted right out of it. Walking over to the Jacuzzi, she placed her wine on the edge and stepped into the hot soothing water. Reaching over, she turned the dial as Philip told her to do and the jets sprang to life. Taking her wine glass in one hand, she gently allowed herself to be absorbed by the powerful jets and felt the tension of the day slide right off her. Stasha thought to herself, *Why did I never purchase one of these?*

Downstairs, Philip dialed Marcel's number. Marcel answered and it sounded like Philip woke him up. "Marcel, its Philip. Sorry if I woke you up. I know that it's late, but I have to talk to you now."

Marcel could hear the urgency in Philip's voice and came completely awake. "Philip let me take the extension downstairs. I don't want to wake Monique."

Philip waited for Marcel to go downstairs to get the other phone. He hated to call Marcel with every event that had happened, but this man, in Philip's opinion, had the right to know because it was his daughter that it was happening to.

"Ok, Philip, tell me what has happened because I can hear it in your voice. Is Stasha ok?"

"Yes, she's fine and she will be staying with me until we find this son of a bitch. He broke into her apartment today. Mary told us that she was there earlier and everything was fine, so it must have happened after she left." Philip then told Marcel everything that had happened up to the point of bringing her to his place. If Marcel didn't like the fact that she would be staying with him, well, Philip didn't care at this point. "We have to bring this guy down. I filled in the investigator and his team with what we're working on and that this may not be just your ordinary break-in. I also asked him if he could look back in Stasha's file to see if they missed anything the last time. They thought that it would be best if she stayed out of the apartment, and then proceeded with a full investigation."

Marcel thought it was a good idea too. The project that Stasha created would be worth millions if it went through. Plus, it would give people the chance of early detection. "I'll see what I can do from here. Do you need anymore men?" Marcel wanted an army watching her, but he knew that was not to be. If anything happened to her, he didn't know how he would survive it.

"No, this time I'm going to take care of it. If it's the last thing I do, I'm going to find out who this is. I'll call you with the reports as I go. Talk to you soon." Philip hung up the phone and put his head in his hands. The question that kept going through his mind was, *who*? He had to find him because, after tonight, he knew the guy had another target in mind and Philip would be damned if he would let him get it. Picking up the towel that he left beside him while talking to Marcel, he went upstairs to see how Stasha was doing. He stood at the bathroom door and leaned against the entry and just took in the sight in front of him. There was Stasha with her head leaning back against the tub with a smile on her lips. Philip could tell that it was exactly what she needed. He walked over to the side of the tub and picked up the face cloth that he left on the side for her. He wished that he had some nice soap for her, but it was the first time he ever had a woman here. He made a mental note to pick some up tomorrow. Leaning down, he gave her a kiss on her lips.

"Hmmm, if I would have known that you had this here, I would have insisted that I came here instead of you coming to my place all the time," Stasha told him. Opening her eyes, she looked up at him as he sat on the side of the tub.

"I see that you're feeling less tense. Sit up and I'll wash your back for you." Stasha didn't need to be told twice. Once she sat up, Philip put the washcloth into the water and then grabbed the soap and lathered it up. Applying light pressure, he began to wash away the remaining stress she may have had. Stasha was enjoying being pampered, and she didn't realize what Philip was up to until he moved the wash cloth to the front and started rubbing her breast with it. She laid back and gave him access to what he desired. Philip knew that she was getting aroused by the soft moans she let escape from her lips. Rinsing her off, he knew that just that action had left him wanting also. Reaching into the tub, he picked her up and carried her into the bedroom. Standing her on the rug in front of the bed, he then took the towel he brought and began to dry her off. He turned her so that her back was to him and began to dry her back first. As he dried her shoulders, he kissed each one. Where the towel went, he made sure to give each curve proper attention. He loved the shape of her bottom. Firm, but still enough to hold on to, and her legs went on forever. Philip turned her around and started drying the front. He could see that Stasha's eyes were already glazed with passion, but he knew the best was yet to come. As he dried her breasts, he took each one into his mouth and suckled just a bit. Moving down to her stomach, he gave a light kiss to her belly button. When he reached the juncture between her legs, he knew that he needed to have her now. Throwing the towel aside, he picked her up and placed her on the bed. Removing his sweat pants, he joined her.

Stasha loved how he made every time special; she always wanted to make sure that he received the same attention. As they lay there looking into each other's eyes, she could tell that what he just did to her was affecting him in the same way. Stasha moved onto her side and started to trail her fingers softly over his chest. She kissed his neck as her fingers trailed down his chest, looking for the one thing she craved to be inside of her, and then she kissed him with a deepness that went to her very core. Tingles went through her body and she knew that she had to have him soon. Feeling the thickness of him, she trailed her fingers down the length of him and then brought them back up to the top. Philip knew that she liked to give as much as she took and he wanted to enjoy what she was doing to him. Her fingers felt like feathers trailing over his body and she could feel that he was more than ready for her.

Philip couldn't take anymore; with one swift move, he had Stasha lying on her back and plunged into the warmth he craved. No other woman made him feel like this. As they peaked to climax, Philip wrapped her in his arms and let the ride take them both. As they lay there in the aftermath of their lovemaking, Philip held her against him. They talked about what happened with the apartment and asked her to be extra careful at work. She reminded him that she always left early anyway. He was going to arrange for a car to bring her and pick her up from work.

To get off the subject, she asked him, "Why haven't you ever invited me here before?"

"Working for my grandfather wasn't as easy as many thought it was for me. He was very hard on me because he knew one day I would be a very rich man. He was wise and told me about the women in his life. After my grandmother died, women seemed to attach themselves to him to gain what came with being with a rich man. He told me that if he dated a woman, he never brought her home. He said that home was for the wife and children, and he loved the memories he still had of my grandmother. He felt uncomfortable bringing a woman home that he wasn't sure would stay. I liked the concept that he had and, until now, I have never brought anyone here. I wanted the woman who walked through that door to be the one I planned to marry."

Stasha sat up and turned to look at him. "I'm sorry that you broke this vow. If my apartment wasn't broken into, we would be laying in my bed instead of yours."

Philip could see the sadness form in Stasha's eyes. Philip put his arms around her and pulled her back down against him. "Stasha, the woman that walked through that door tonight is the woman that I plan to marry, that's if she'll have me."

Stasha felt the tears start to run down her cheeks as she just realized that Philip asked her to marry him. "You see, Stasha, I didn't believe it could happen so quickly, but seeing you in that airport that day, I knew that the woman who looked at me so intently was the woman that I was going to marry. Then I realized that, even though I might not have met you at the wedding, you will recall, we did have a meeting set up to meet afterwards at work. So you see, fate would have brought us together anyway."

Stasha knew that what he said was true. Fate would have brought them together.

Philip got up and walked over to his armoire and opened the top drawer. Coming back to bed, he held in his hand a small gold box. "Before I open this box, Stasha, I want you to know that I will always be here for you. If you agree to be my wife, I will always love you."

Stasha sat beside him and watched as Philip opened the tiny box. Stasha gasped when she saw what it held inside. There, nestled on white velvet was the most beautiful ring she had ever seen. It wasn't large like most women would expect. It had a single diamond with a gold design that went all the way around. It was very simple, but so very elegant. Looking up into Philip eyes, Stasha said, "Philip, it is so beautiful. Yes, I would love to be your wife and I promise to always love you and be here for you also."

Philip took the ring out and took her hand in his. Slipping the ring on her finger felt so right to him. "This ring has special meaning for me. My grandfather told me when I make the right choice and finally find the woman who would be my wife, that I should give this to her. It was my grandmother's, my grandfather told me that the day he placed this ring on her finger; a day never went past that they didn't love each other. She always told him that it was the most precious thing he'd given her besides their child." Philip added, "Being in the position that I'm in, most women expect the best of everything and that was not what I was looking for. I wanted someone who appreciated the small things in life and you do."

Stasha knew that the tears were running down her cheeks so fast. He was the type of man she wished she would eventually find. He was so caring and thoughtful. Lying back down in bed and snuggling up to him, she admired her ring as they started to talk about their future together. As it got later into the night, Philip and Stasha held each other and drifted off.

CHAPTER 15

Walking into work the next day, Stasha was all smiles. Sitting at her desk, she waited for Tara to come in with the coffee that they shared every morning while they went through her schedule for the day. When Tara came in, Stasha made a point of grabbing her mug with her left hand. Tara saw the ring and then looked up at Stasha.

"Is this what I think it is?" she asked Stasha.

"He asked me last night," she replied with a huge grin on her face.

Tara came around the desk and gave her a hug. "I'm so happy for you. So have you picked a date yet?"

Stasha sat back and took a sip of her coffee. "No, we have so much going on with the project that we decided to wait to make a date after it is shipped off for approval."

Tara was so happy for her boss because she had seen what Eric had done to her. These last few months with Philip made her so happy. After they finished going through the morning routine, Tara went back to her desk to get caught up on her memos that needed to go out by that afternoon.

Stasha still couldn't believe that she was engaged. Picking up the phone, she dialed a number that she had known since she was a little girl. When her father picked up, she was so excited to give him the great news. "Hi Dad, how is your day going so far?" she asked him trying to keep the excitement out of her voice.

"Good, but I have a couple of meetings this afternoon with some new clients interested in using our company. How are things with you?"

Stasha sat back and gave him the news. "Well, to start with, I had to move in with Philip because when we arrived home yesterday my apartment had been broken into. So if you need to get a hold of me you can call me there. Do you have his number? They want to do an investigation because the detective thinks that it may have something to do with the project Philip and I have been working on. Oh, also, I wanted to tell you that Philip and I are engaged!" Stasha wanted to string the conversation on a bit more before she told him, but found that she just couldn't do it.

"That's great honey. He phoned me and asked for my blessing last week, but I didn't think that he was going to ask you so soon." Marcel was so happy that his daughter found a good man. He never did like Eric, but he kept out of it because he did not want to have Stasha angry with him. "So, have you set a date?" he asked. He would be so proud to walk her down the aisle. The only other thing he wished she would have that special day would be for her mother to be there. "No, Dad, we're going to wait until we have the project off and running before we set a date. I don't really mind because we have only been together such a short while and this will give us time to get to know more about each other. Dad, I plan to only marry once," she told him. The nice thing about her father was that she could always be honest with him and he never judged her.

"Well, honey, I just want you to know that I'm very happy for you and I know that you and Philip will be very happy together. Stasha, I hope you know that I will always stand by you in any decisions that you make; if down the road you feel this is not for you, I will be there for you."

Stasha knew that she was lucky to have a father like him.

Marcel couldn't wait to tell the rest of the family. Monique would probably want to get started right away with plans. That will be the hardest part for him. She would want to get started right away, but he would have to hold her off for a while. "Did Philip tell his family yet? If Monique can't start on any plans for the wedding, she will at least want to get together with the LaRochs' to celebrate," Marcel said.

"Yes, Dad, I believe he was calling them this morning and you could tell Monique that if she wants to put some plans to paper then we will look them over when we come home again." Stasha was happy that both of their families knew each other and got along well. "Ok,

Dad, I better let you go. I still have to tell Franny the good news and you know I will be on the phone with her for a while; plus, if I want to make my meetings this afternoon, I better do it now. Love you, and I'll talk to you soon."

Hanging up the phone, Stasha looked at the clock to see what time it was. She knew that Franny had taken the day off today and didn't want to wake her if she was still sleeping. Dialing her number, she decided to see if she could make lunch. That way, they would have an hour to talk. "Hi Franny, hope I didn't wake you, but I thought that if you're free for lunch, I need to talk to you about something."

Franny told her that it would be great and that she would meet her at the restaurant down the street from her office at one o'clock.

Stasha knew that Franny was going to be so excited when she asked her to be her Maid of Honor. She couldn't think of anyone else she wanted by her side. Stasha got a lot of work done and was surprised to look at the clock and see that it was already time to leave for lunch. Picking up her purse, she closed her office door and informed Tara that she would be back around two. Stasha decided to walk because the day was so warm and the restaurant was only a block away. Arriving at the restaurant, she sat down at a table and ordered a club soda and lemon and informed the waiter that she was waiting for someone.

Franny showed up a few minutes later and took the seat opposite of Stasha. "Is anything wrong?" Franny asked after the waiter left with their order.

Stasha had kept her hand on her lap and said, "Yes, I want to show you something and see what your reaction is. I hope that you can help me with this situation."

Franny was a little worried now because Stasha was always good at figuring things out for herself. Occasionally, she would bounce stuff off her to see what her opinion would be. "Sure, Stasha, you know I'll help you with anything, shoot."

Stasha took her hand out from under the table and showed Franny her ring. Franny's jaw dropped when she saw the ring and grabbed Stasha's hand toward her to get a better look. "Oh my god!"

Franny yelled out loud, making a few people in the restaurant turn to see what the commotion was all about. "When did this happen? And why didn't you call me?" Franny asked her.

"Well, the reason why I didn't call you is because he just asked me last night and I wanted to tell you in person; I also want you to be my Maid of Honor. I want my best friend there, Fran."

Franny started to cry, which started tears to form in Stasha's eyes. Coming around the table, Franny gave her a big hug and told her that she would love to be her Maid of Honor and nothing would stop her from doing so.

During lunch, Stasha told her how he had proposed and had them in tears again. She also said what kind of things they would like to look at for the wedding. Stasha told her that they were going to wait a while, but it wouldn't hurt to work on some ideas. She asked her about Brad and Franny told her that she hadn't called him yet because she didn't want to seem too forward.

"I'll call him later in the week and see what he is up to this weekend. I have an early shift Saturday and changed with someone for the afternoon shift on Sunday."

They talked about how much fun it had been to go home for the holiday and see everyone. Stasha was glad to see Jean- Paul, Andre, and Tina. They both laughed over how Jean -Paul used to be on them about every little thing they did, then to see how two small girls, ages two and four, had him wrapped around their little fingers. Andre looked good, but they could tell that he was tired. Parliament had just broke for summer and he had worked long days trying to catch up on it. Tina had just opened her own Salon and Spa and both Franny and Stasha took time to go see it. It was very chic and catered to the very wealthy in Montreal. Franny's family was so glad to have her home for the long weekend and made sure that they got as much as possible into those four days.

Stasha's cell phone started to ring; looking at the call display, she noticed that it was Philip. "Hi Philip, I'm just having lunch with Franny and told her our good news. Philip says hello and wants to know what spell you put on his buddy. Apparently, Brad can't get any work done."

At this, Franny laughed and assured Stasha that no spells were needed.

Stasha laughed and told Philip, who laughed along with them. Philip asked her when she would be back at the office because he wanted her to look at some things that came up in the testing and needed to see what she thought.

"I will be leaving in a few minutes. Ok, I'll see you there." Hanging up the phone, she paid the bill and told Franny, who was arguing with her about it, that she could get the next one. Franny agreed and walked back with Stasha to her building. Outside Stasha's building, Franny told her that she would be working all week and would call her to tell her how her weekend went. Arriving at her office, she noticed that Tara was not at her desk. Stasha sat down at her desk and began to read the papers that would be needed at her meeting with a company they used in the past for special equipment designs and to make sure that they saw the changes she had made. A yellow envelope was sticking out of her papers and she picked it up. Tearing the seal, she took out the piece of paper and read it. Instantly, she dropped it on her desk and backed away. Shock was all she could feel right now and that was how Philip found her.

"Stasha, what's wrong?" He could see things were not right and she looked down and pointed to the letter.

"I thought that it was part of the mail and maybe got mixed up in my papers."

Philip turned the paper over with a pen so he could read it without touching it. "Stasha, I hope you liked what I did with your apartment. I warned you that I wanted the project dropped, but you just don't listen. See how close I can get to you. I'll be nice and give you another chance. "KILL THE PROJECT" or your new boyfriend will have to find someone else to love." Philip read the note and was seeing red. That son of a bitch had to be stopped. Philip called the detective that was on the case and told him about the letter.

The detective said he was going to come down and pick it up. He hoped that he could get a print; if was done on a computer, the printer would give them something because they were all unique. While they waited for the detective to arrive, they moved over to the couch and went over the findings they had done on the project. Stasha was happy that things were going well: the note and the phone calls were not going to stop her now. This was her dream and she was so close to having it become a reality. The investigator showed up and took Stasha's prints so they could eliminate them from the envelope.

After the detective left, Philip told her that, if everything went well with the test they performed tomorrow, they would be able to have it shipped out for the government to do the final testing. That process could take years, but less than a year if they were lucky. Both Philip and Stasha were hopping for the lesser of the two. Now that they had gone this far, they were confident that either way, one day they would be able to help people have a device that could actually help them in the long run.

"I have a late meeting tonight so I'll see you when I get home. The car will be here to pick you up at five thirty." Philip gave her a kiss and, while walking out of her office, wished that he could rearrange his schedule. He didn't feel good about leaving her right now.

Tara came in to tell her that her meeting was set up in the board room and that everyone had arrived. Stasha picked up her papers and both Tara and she walked there in silence. Tara saw the detective come and knew that if Stasha needed to tell her anything, she would do so. The rest of the day went very well and now it was time to pack up for the day. The car was out front. As Stasha got in, she thought about how it was going to feel walking into Philip's place alone. He had given her the extra card for the elevator that morning. Riding up the elevator, Stasha really didn't know what Philip wanted to do once they married. Would they stay here or buy a house? Stasha knew that if they had children she would prefer to have a house, where they would have a backyard for the children to play in. Also, a place where they could entertain guests for outdoor barbeques.

As she opened the door, she still couldn't believe how big his place really was. Putting her purse on the table, she walked over to the bar and poured herself a glass of wine. Philip said that he would be late, so Stasha walked into the kitchen and looked in the fridge.

Philip's kitchen had a lot of room. The cupboards were a dark cherry and the counter was a black, speckled marble. All the appliances were stainless steel, but the overall effect wasn't dark at all. For someone who lived on his own, his fridge was well stocked. Stasha decided that, since she had a big lunch with Franny, she would just make a salad. Taking all the vegetables out, she brought them over to the island that was centered in the middle. Stasha always liked middle islands. Philip's had a double sink in it and a solid wood block that was set in the marble. After washing the vegetables, she chopped them up and tossed them in the bowl she found in one of the cupboards. Peeking to see if he had anything to garnish it with, Stasha found a seasoning mixture that would do. Taking her salad and wine, she went into the living room, sat down on the couch, and, after a few minutes, figured out how to use the remote for the television. Munching on her salad, Stasha curled up in the corner and watched the news. After finishing her supper, she went into the kitchen to clean up. Once everything was done, she filled her wine glass and decided that she would try out the Jacuzzi again. Just as she was walking upstairs, the phone rang. She went over and answered it. "Demonde residence."

"Hi Stasha," Philip said. He was glad that she was safe. "I'm finished with the meeting and I'm on my way home. Do you need me to pick up anything?"

She was glad that he was on his way home. "No thanks, I just had a salad. Do you want me to fix you something before I get in the bath?"

Philip told her not to worry about it. He would make something when he got there. "I'm glad that you're enjoying my bathtub. Maybe you could save me some room and I'll join you."

Stasha laughed and promised him that she would make some space for him if he was still up to it. Hanging up, she went upstairs and put her wine on the side and adjusted the water so that it would be just right. Walking into the bedroom, she removed her suit and placed it aside so she could drop it off at the dry cleaners tomorrow. Going into the bathroom, Stasha stepped into the tub and just let the hot water seep into her sore muscles. She thought about how long it had been since she had worked out and hoped that she could get back into her old routine soon. She had just turned on the jets when she heard Philip call up to her that he was home. Sipping her wine, she laid her head back and enjoyed the pulsating motion that the jets supplied.

Philip came in about twenty minutes later and joined her in the tub. Stepping in, he sat so that Stasha could lean her back against his chest. He picked up her glass and took a drink of wine. Closing his eyes, he told her, "I think that I could get used to coming home to this."

Stasha turned and kissed him. "Did you talk to your parents today?"

Philip told her that he did call, like he promised her this morning, and they were very happy to hear the news. His mother couldn't wait to start getting plans together and mentioned that she would need to speak to Monique as soon as possible.

"Did you happen to tell your mother that we are going to wait?"

Philip nodded; he knew from his mother's voice that she was sad about that. He told her that she could help them by getting some plans together and seemed happier after that.

"Don't worry, Philip. I'm sure that Monique and my dad have already called them. Dad wanted to get together with them so they could celebrate for us. We just won't be there. Also, I told Dad that Monique could start putting some ideas together and that we would look them over when we went there again."

Philip was glad that they figured out how to make sure that both mothers would be satisfied, even if they couldn't do it right away.

By the time they got out of the tub, it was late. Drying off, they both walked into the bedroom and climbed into bed. Philip held her in his arms; as they fell asleep, he vowed to himself that he would never let any harm come to her.

CHAPTER 16

Three weeks had passed and Stasha was finally able to concentrate on the other projects that had been started for Magna, and the work kept her busy. Philip was busy himself and it seemed that the only time they saw each other was at night. Two weeks ago, they had a party for everyone involved with the project. It had been sent out for its government approval that day. Stasha knew it could take a long time, but with all the testing that had been done in their own labs; they hoped it would go quicker for the government to approve it. That night, they thanked everyone who helped bring the dream to fruition. Now, both Philip and Stasha would go through the agony of hoping that it would pass.

Philip had been glad that the phone calls had stopped and there had been no other letters to Stasha. He still didn't like the idea that there was some sick person out there who could hurt her. The one thing that kept coming to his mind was why didn't this guy come after him. He was a part of getting the project off for approval. He started to make a list of everything that had happened so far. The detective on the case was still going through all the evidence that they retrieved from the apartment. Philip had had a few meetings out of town while everything with the apartment and the letter had been happening and had to reschedule. At that time, he was not going to let her be alone. Now, he needed to make up those appointments and would have to leave next week. After work, he stopped at Stasha's office to pick her up. Being a partner in the company, her office had been moved to a larger one. Seeing Tara still at her desk, Philip inquired if Stasha was still in her office. He didn't want to go in because the door was closed and she could be with a client.

"Yes, she is. You can go in Mr. Demonde; she finished her last meeting about a half hour ago."

Philip thanked her and walked into Stasha's office. Looking at her sitting there at her desk, he could tell that she was tired. "Is there a lady in here who would like to go home?" At the sound of his voice, Stasha raised her head and smiled at him. Philip picked her up after work when he had the time. "Hi there, let me just finish this up and I'll be right with you." Philip walked over to the window and looked out. It was still daylight and she had a perfect view.

Stasha put all the papers she had been looking over away in their file and straightened up her desk. "Ok, let's get out of here." She went to her closet that looked like one of her walls and opened it up. It was nice to have because if anyone walked into the office, they wouldn't know it was even there.

"Do you want to pick up something or go to a restaurant for supper?" he asked her.

It was Friday and, even though Stasha was tired, they had spent so many evenings in that going out would be a nice change. "Let's go out. It's been so long since we have."

That being decided, Philip drove to a quiet restaurant he knew not far from the office. Arriving at the restaurant, there was no problem getting a table without a reservation. As they were seated, Philip told her, "That is the only advantage of being known in this city."

Stasha laughed because she knew that he did not show off like other well off people. His life was very private and he seemed to like it that way. He didn't mind too much when their engagement showed up in the paper; Stasha knew that it might happen. Being engaged to one of the richest men in New York was news.

After they ordered, Philip told her that there were meetings that he had put off, but couldn't delay anymore. "I will be leaving on Monday and should be back by Friday. Are you going to be ok while I'm gone?"

Stasha knew that what had happened recently really bothered Philip, but she had to make sure that he knew that his going out of town would not bother her. "I'm fine with that, Philip. You have your work to do and I'm a big girl, remember?"

Philip thought to himself, *I definitely know that you're a big girl.* A smile appeared on his face that made Stasha laugh.

"Plus, your building is one of the most secure buildings in the city." That was why Philip picked the place. He didn't want reporters and anyone else having easy access to his life.

"Promise me that while I'm gone that you won't stay late at work."

Stasha knew that it was important to him, so she agreed that she wouldn't. Supper was nice, and feeling relaxed was something Stasha needed. She had a few new clients that she would be meeting with next week and had been going over the information they sent her. It was important to her that they picked her firm to work with on these various projects.

Letting themselves in the apartment, Philip went to the bar and poured them both a glass of wine. Since being with Stasha, he had acquired a taste for the stuff. He also liked the fact that it eased some of the tension at the end of the day. He handed her a glass and sat down beside her. "Have you had anymore of those dreams lately?"

Stasha hadn't, and she thought it was because she was sleeping with Philip beside her; she felt safe and that was the reason they haven't returned. "No I haven't, but believe me, if I did you would be the first to know. My dad told me that when he stayed with me after what happened, I would scream and I knew that with the last two I had, I woke in a cold sweat."

They sat and watched television for a while, and then decided to turn in for the night. "Oh, Brad called me today and asked if you and I would like to join Franny and him for supper tomorrow. He doesn't want to make Franny uneasy about their first date and thought that if we were there she might feel more comfortable."

Stasha smiled at Philip and told him that it would be fine with her. In the back of her mind, she thought Franny would be more than happy to be alone with him, but it was sweet how Brad thought of her this way.

"I'll call him tomorrow morning and tell him," Philip said. They both slept in till ten o'clock the next morning. Philip told Stasha that he was going to go for a run and would be back in about an hour. Stasha didn't mind and ate her breakfast while reading the morning paper. Cleaning up afterwards, she headed for the shower. She wanted to do some shopping today. It had been a long time since she bought something for herself. Philip walked in the door just as she came downstairs.

"Where are you off to this morning?" Philip asked. He hated the fact that some guy was out there and he hadn't found anything on him yet, and Stasha wanted to go out by herself.

"I'm going downtown to do some shopping. I have been cooped up for so long that I haven't gone shopping in a while. I want to pick up something that I can wear tonight when we go for supper with Brad and Franny." Giving him a kiss, she picked up her purse and waved to him as she went out the door.

Philip knew that he couldn't shield her like he wanted. He knew that one of their men would follow her to make sure she stayed safe. With that thought, he headed up to the bathroom and took a shower. The run had felt good and relieved some of the stress that had built up over the last few weeks. Philip had talked to Brad about everything that had been going on and Brad said that he would talk to Franny about the man Stasha used to date. Eric worked in the same hospital as Franny, and Philip wanted to know if Eric had been asking Franny any questions about Stasha lately. Brad said that he would talk to him tonight about what he found out.

Franny worked till three and he was going to pick her up around six. They were going to meet at the restaurant around seven. Philip figured that he and Brad would be able to get some time in to talk. Philip went into the kitchen and made himself a sandwich of Montreal smoked meat and Dijon mustard and grabbed a beer. He went to see what game was on television. It wasn't too often that he stayed home and didn't work on Saturdays, but since he had made the decision with Stasha to take Saturdays off, he thought he could get some game time in. He loved soccer and sat back to watch the game between Italy and the States. He played soccer in university and knew that it could get rough.

Just as the game finished, with Italy as the winning team, Stasha walked in the door. "I see that you took our talk to heart and had a good day." Stasha liked to see him relaxed, and with the couple of beer cans and the bag of chips on the table, she knew that a sport had to have been involved. Franny's brothers were the same way.

Philip got up and started clearing up his mess as he watched Stasha bring in her bags. "I hope that you left something in the stores," he said with a laugh. Stasha laughed also because the weight of the bags were heavy, but she had the best time. She picked up a beautiful black dress for dinner with black strapped shoes. There were also a couple of outfits she thought would be nice for work and a velour track suit that she could wear on their days just staying home. Stasha put everything away and started to get ready for dinner. Taking her brush, she styled her hair in a neat French twist and had left some of her bangs to lay over to the side. A few tendrils were left to enhance her neck. The dress fit her every curve and, looking in the mirror, she was glad she had bought it. She never usually spent that much on a dress, but decided to splurge on herself.

As she was putting on her pearl earrings, Philip came up from behind and put his arms around her waist. "Hmmm, if I knew that I would walk in here to see this beautiful woman in my bedroom, I should have told Brad we were busy.

Stasha smiled, and then said, "No way, Philip, I just finished getting ready and you better hurry if we are to meet them for drinks."

Philip laughed and swatted her behind as he went to the closet to get the suit that he would wear tonight.

Stasha liked the fact that he could pick out his own clothes. Eric never did and would complain if she picked something that he didn't feel like wearing. Philip showered and got dress. It was six o'clock when they left the apartment.

Arriving at the restaurant, Philip and Stasha told the *maitre d'* that they were to join Brad and Fran. He informed them that they had not arrived yet and would they care to go into the lounge while they waited for their friends.

"I will inform them when they arrive where you are."

Philip thanked him and walked Stasha over to a chair. The tables were set in the lounge for comfort; four chairs were set around a very nicely decorated table. In the middle sat a small candle that gave just enough light to make the mood romantic. After ordering drinks, Stasha and Philip started to talk about the wedding.

"Are you sure that you want to wait," Philip asked her with a small smile.

"Well, I would like to make sure that everything is going well with the project because when I start looking into the wedding arrangements, I don't want to be distracted."

Philip would get married tomorrow if he had it his way. He didn't want to lose her now that he had found her. "How about if we set a date?" he asked her.

"Ok, I do have a date in mind; how about June 20. It's supposed to be the longest day of the year and I want our wedding day to last as long as possible."

Philip thought it was a great idea. He was happy that the date was set too. Since his mom found out about the engagement, she had called him to ask if it was set. Now, he could give her a date. They had discussed that they would let their moms gather some ideas, and then sit down with them to see which ones they preferred. With both of their busy schedules, they knew that it would put to much pressure on them. Since they would be married in Montreal, they thought to leave it to the experts.

Brad and Franny arrived a few minutes after and joined them for a drink. Franny put in a full shift but she looked great. After they finished their drinks, the *maitre d'* came over and escorted them to their table.

Dinner was nice. Stasha was glad that Franny had been given the chance to meet Brad. He was very intelligent, but didn't push the subject of work. After supper, Brad and Philip excused themselves. Philip told Stasha that Brad was looking into something for him and would only take a minute.

Stasha started telling Franny all the good buys she found that day while Philip and Brad went into the bar and ordered a drink.

"So, did you find out anything from Franny?" Philip asked him.

"When we talked on the phone last night, I steered the conversation towards work and Franny told me about Eric. She said that when Stasha was seeing him, she did run the idea across to him and Franny. She told me that he just laughed it off. She told me it made Stasha so angry because he informed her to stick to things that she knew about. After they split up, Eric used to ask Franny a lot of questions about Stasha and what projects she was working on. Franny got so annoyed with him that she told him to mind his own business." Brad laughed after this comment. Brad also told him that he checked to see if Eric was anyway involved with what had happened three years ago, but, because he was one of the top cancer doctors in the States, they went easy on him.

Philip thought that they would be on to something, but it seemed like a dead end. Even if it was Eric, how would he have gotten the information about what Stasha was doing if Franny wasn't giving him any? Philip asked Brad if he could do some more checking on this. "Someone has to know something. The person behind all this knew that we were ready to send it off."

Brad told him he would ask a few associates who happened to be around when it all went down. There was one person who he couldn't reach because he was on vacation when he called him. "He should be back before Friday." Philip reminded him that he needed to go to those meetings that he put off. Brad didn't need to go with him and Philip asked him if he wouldn't mind checking on Stasha while he was gone. After Brad agreed, both men thought that they had better get back to their ladies.

After leaving the restaurant, they decided to do some dancing at the club not too far away. By one o'clock, Stasha and Philip called it a night. Franny promised to call her during the week. With a wave goodbye, they headed for home.

Opening the door for her, Stasha went to put her purse on the table. "I don't think that I've stayed out so late in years. I had the best time. If I knew you could dance like that, I would have asked you to take me dancing more often," Stasha told him. After making sure everything was locked up for the evening, hand in hand they walked up stairs.

"I could definitely get used to having Saturdays off," Philip said. Taking off his jacket, he watched as Stasha took off her earrings and undid her hair. It swept down her back. Walking over to her, he turned her around to undo her zipper. As the straps fell over her shoulders, he kissed each one softly. Letting the dress fall to the floor, he turned her around and cupped one of her breasts in his hand. He loved the weight that filled his palm. Sweeping her hair off her shoulder, he kissed her neck.

Stasha loved the way he gave attention to everything he did in their lovemaking. Tingles swept through her whole body. Walking over to the bed, he gently laid her down. Starting with one of her legs, he removed her shoe and then did the same with the other. Placing them on the floor, he then removed her nylons.

The tiny lace black panties she wore underneath almost drove him over the edge, but he held himself in check. He wanted her to enjoy this as much as he was. He started at her toes and proceeded to massage her feet and moved up her legs.

Stasha loved how his hands felt on her skin. He took care of them; they didn't feel harsh. Philip had wanted to do this since he walked in the room before they left for supper. Looking at her in that dress all evening was torture. When he reached the top of her thighs, he slipped his fingers under the side of her panties and drew them off her. Standing there and looking at her while she lay on his bed, the passion so clearly visible in her eyes was more than he could take.

Stasha knew that he had reached his point of no return when he started to take his clothes off. She loved to see how his muscles would bunch with every movement he made as he undressed.

Philip walked over to the bed and lay down beside her. He played with her breast with soft movements; until he saw the perfect peaks come to attention. Letting his fingertips move down her body, he led a path to where he desperately wanted to be. Taking his finger, he played with the little bud until he could feel it swell.

Stasha didn't fight the feeling that was building inside of her. She wanted him inside her and giving her the release that she knew he could bring. She couldn't take anymore and rolled on top of him. Sitting astride, she reached between her legs and took him in her hands and directed him to the place she needed him to be. Slowly, she sank down upon him; feeling him inside was wonderful. Stasha started to raise herself almost to the point of releasing him and then slipped back down so that he was impaled to the hilt. As Stasha continued to take what she wanted, Philip held back as long as he could.

After a few more movements, he couldn't take no more. He lifted her up and turned her so that she lay underneath him. Philip pumped into her with a feverish pitch. When the release came, they both screamed out together. Laying there in the aftermath, both tried to get their breath back. Philip opened his eyes to see Stasha with hers still closed. He lifted himself off her and lay down beside her.

"I don't think I will ever tire of this," she told him once she opened her eyes and looked at him. Philip felt the same way. Stasha cuddled up next to him and asked him, "So what time is your flight on Monday?"

Philip didn't want to talk about work, "I'm scheduled for a six a.m. flight. I'll try to be as quiet as I can so I don't wake you." He decided to pack the next day so that he would have his luggage by the door.

The next day, they lingered over coffee and the paper. After lunch, they decided to take a walk through the park. It was sunny and warm. Walking hand in hand, they watched as some parents ran after their little ones. Stasha thought that in a couple of years that could be them.

It was supper time by the time they got back and Stasha went in the kitchen to prepare supper. She had put chicken breast in the fridge to marinate while they were gone. She fixed up a salad and prepared the asparagus. They had gone by the bakery on the way back and Stasha ran in to get some fresh buns. She made rice in a chicken broth. As it cooked, she went out into the living room to pour herself a glass of wine. Going back into the kitchen, she took the plates out of the cupboard and set the table. They ate in the kitchen most of the time; with just the two of them there, it made no sense to eat at the dinning room table.

Philip finished packing and brought his luggage downstairs. He went over to the bar and poured himself a glass of wine and went to join Stasha in the kitchen.

"All ready to go?" Stasha asked him as soon as she saw him come into the kitchen.

Philip looked in the oven and turned around. "Yes, I have everything by the door. Are you sure you're going to be o.k. while I'm gone?"

She walked over to him and put her arms around his neck. "Yes, I will be just fine while you're gone. You promised to call me every day and I promised not to stay at work to late. Plus, you're only going till Friday." She kissed him and went to get supper on the table.

After supper, Philip helped her clean up and then they went to watch a movie they rented that afternoon. Philip needed to go to bed early, so they decided that right after supper they would watch it. Philip poured them another glass of wine and they sat cuddled up on the couch to watch it. It was an action movie and Philip mentioned that he had never seen it. Stasha had picked out a love story, and then decided that they could watch her movie the next time they rented one. In one part of the movie, Philip had to explain to Stasha how the one guy's nose busted so easy by the way the good guy held his hand. "One good hit and you're sure to break it," Philip told her. They called it an early night and went to bed. The next morning, Philip had gotten up without waking Stasha and got ready. Walking over to the bed, he kissed her on the cheek and whispered goodbye. Philip went down stairs and picked up his luggage and slipped out the door.

CHAPTER 17

Stasha heard Philip leave. Sitting up in bed, she knew that Philip was more worried than he let on. Showing her how to break someone's nose was what gave it away. Stasha had known for quite some time that her father had had someone watching her. He was there when she woke up in the hospital and saw how angry he was at what had happened. After her mom died, he had vowed to her to keep her safe and Marcel Monteau never went back on a promise. Stasha knew the time had come to tell him that she knew he had her followed, and also to take a stand for herself. Everyone thought that she always needed protection; they needed to see that she wasn't so soft.

It was early, but Stasha figured there was no sense lying in bed any longer and went to take a shower. She dressed in a gray pinstriped pant suit with a white silk blouse underneath. She had seen it the day she went shopping and thought it would be a good power suit to wear at the office when conducting meetings with the new clients. The types of people Magna dealt with needed reassurance from the company that they put their projects into. As long as they felt that the person in charge knew what they expected and could work with them, then they would sign the contract. It was up to Stasha to make sure that those contracts got signed. Tom had been enjoying his time off and now came in periodically to see how things were going. Sitting in front of the mirror, she applied her make-up and twisted her hair up in a French twist. Having her hair highlighted the other day to a lighter blond gave her look a softer edge. Going downstairs, she poured herself a cup of coffee and added a couple of slices of rye bread to the toaster. While waiting for her toast to be done, Stasha sat at the table to read the newspaper. The toast popped up and Stasha added a small amount of cheese to it and sat back down to finish reading the paper. It had been a long time for her to be able to just sit by herself and linger over the paper. Turning the pages, she came across the elite section. She liked to see who had given to the many charities and who preened in front of the camera because they attended a fundraiser event. Stasha had been to quiet a few of those herself with her father. Marcel didn't mind having his picture taken, but tried to avoid it as much as possible.

He had told her once that the people who preen for the cameras need the attention, and he didn't need the attention. He enjoyed giving money to charities but only the ones he checked out first. Marcel gave a very large amount each year and made sure that the money went directly to the people that needed it. Only once did he trust a charity that ended up using his money for office help and not for the cause. He made sure it never happened again. Turning the page over, Stasha sat there and stared at the picture in front of her. It was Eric at an awards banquet. Stasha couldn't really see the woman with him because she was turned away from the camera. She did look familiar though. It said in the article that Eric had been presented with an award for the compassion and time spent with cancer patients. Stasha remembered that, even though he was strict with her, he did give a lot to his patients. She remembered how they had talked about her dream to make something that would help people the same way he did. At the time, he laughed at her. After seeing the article, she was happy that he found someone he could boss around, as long as it wasn't her. She did feel for the poor girl he was with. Eric was the type of person that needed everything done his way. Looking at the clock, Stasha realized that the car to pick her up would be here soon. Taking a last sip of her coffee, she rinsed out the cup and put it and her plate in the dishwasher. Picking up her purse, she turned on the alarm and walked into the elevator. Arriving at work, Stasha noticed that Tara was already there. Walking into her office, she put her purse away in the closet and sat at her desk. Looking at her appointments for the day, she looked up and smiled. Tara always brought their coffee into the office and closed the door. This gave them time to go over everything that needed to be done, and then they had a gab session on what went on during the weekend.

Stasha looked at Tara and thought how sad it was that this beautiful girl had never really had a relationship. Every Monday she would tell Stasha how she stayed home or went to the movies with a girlfriend, but had never mentioned a special guy. Stasha even thought that maybe she wasn't into guys at all. She never asked her because Tara always did the work she was supposed to do and rarely gave Stasha any problems. They worked well together.

"So what did you do this weekend?" Stasha asked before taking a sip of coffee.

Tara looked up and smiled, "I went to a charity fundraiser with a friend. It was very exciting. I had never been before and to see all the people dressed up so elegantly was amazing."

Stasha remembered her first reaction to a gala event. The beauty of it stayed with her for a long time afterwards and she knew that Tara would relive the experience for a while.

Tara got up and went back to her desk to type up some contracts that would be needed for the meetings scheduled for the afternoon. Stasha decided to call her father and have that much needed chat with him. She had to tell him that she knew and to back off a little. He had to realize that she was a big girl now. Dialing his number at home, he didn't go in till the afternoon on Mondays; she waited for someone to pick up. After the fourth ring, Monique answered.

"Hello Monique, its Stasha. By chance, is my dad home?"

"Oh, hello dear, yes he is; just give me a moment and I will get him for you."

Stasha waited a few minutes while Monique went to get her father. In that time, she had to figure out how to start the conversation.

A few minutes later, Marcel came on the line, "Well, hello, it's a nice surprise to hear from my special girl on a Monday morning. How are you doing?" Stasha loved the endearment that he called her. "Hi dad, I have to talk to you about something and I don't want you to get upset. Dad, I know that Ted my doorman has been keeping an eye on me for you." She waited to see what he would say.

Marcel knew that the day would come that he would have to talk to her about this. He tried to keep it quite because he knew that some people didn't appreciate having bodyguards and Stasha had said no to the idea three years ago.

Marcel let out a breath and told her, "I guess I should have known that you would find out. You never seemed afraid to go out after what happened, and here I thought that my men were doing a great job. Honey, you have to understand that I did it for you. When I saw you in the hospital after your attack, it tore me apart. I wanted to put my hands around that bastard's neck and squeeze. I knew that with your memory and not able to recall who it was, I didn't want to take the chance that you could be talking to that person without realizing who it was, and give him another chance to hurt you."

Stasha sat back and took everything in that her father had just said. If it happened to her father or anyone she loved, she probably would have wanted to do the same thing. "Ok, Dad, I understand," she told him.

Marcel felt relief wash over him. He knew that Stasha could be stubborn at times and he didn't want a fight to erupt over something like this. "Stasha, with the apartment being broken into and the letters that you received, could you just let them keep doing their job until we catch this person. We have been working on some leads and I'm sure that we are getting close to finding out who it is." Marcel waited patiently for her reply.

Stasha knew that when he referred to "we," he meant Philip and himself. She had never told her father about the letters, but she told Philip. Philip heard the message on her machine also. "Dad, I have a lot of work coming up at the office. I don't want your men knowing I know because then they will feel that it would be ok to move closer, and you know how I feel about having bodyguards. I can't let anything disrupt the new contracts I have coming into the company over the next few days." Stasha knew that her father would understand the business aspect of it and hoped it would be enough.

"I promise you that they will continue with what their doing now and not interrupt you at work."

Marcel was glad that it finally came out. "So how are things going with you and Philip?" Marcel was proud to tell everyone he knew that his daughter and Philip Demonde were engaged.

"Things are going great. He had to leave on business this week, but will be back on Friday. Tell Monique that once we get some time arranged, we will be down to look over all the plans that she and Jose have gathered together." Stasha told him that she loved him, but had to let him go. She had to get her notes together for her eleven o'clock meeting. After hanging up the phone, Stasha sat back and reflected on what Marcel said. They were getting close. She just wished that her memory would come back so she could end this. Gathering up her notes, she walked out of her office and went to the board room where her new clients from Australia were waiting.

The week seemed to fly by, and Philip called every night to see how she was doing. On Wednesday evening, Philip called around eight to hear a groggy Stasha answer the phone. "Stasha, did I wake you up? It's only eight o'clock, are you ok? Did anything happen that I should know about?" Philip didn't want to sound worried, but he couldn't help it.

"No, I'm fine. I think I caught a cold. This afternoon I felt it coming on, so when I got home I made myself some hot tea with lemon and honey and just laid down on the couch. It will probably be gone by tomorrow. How are things with you?" Stasha sat up on the couch and tried to wake up enough to talk to him.

"Everything is great. The meeting went great and I wrapped up everything this afternoon. I changed my flight to tomorrow instead of Friday. Do you still want me to pick you up from work? If you're up to it, maybe we could even go celebrate the contracts I signed this afternoon for the two major projects that Tantum Laboratories took on." Philip couldn't wait until he got home to tell her. These two projects would open some more doors for the company.

"Oh, Philip, you got them, that's great! We will definitely have to go and celebrate when you come home. I'll just stay at the office and wait for you. It will give me time to do some extra work. I never get to work late anymore. I talked to my dad on Monday concerning my friends that have been keeping an eye out for my father." Stasha wanted to hear his reaction to that.

Philip knew that he had a smart woman and wondered how Marcel kept it from her for so long. "Honey, remember that we love you and your dad just wanted to keep you safe. If I had to keep our children safe, I would do the same thing."

Stasha knew that he was right, but to hear him talk about the both of them having children of their own brought tears to her eyes. "It's ok, Philip. I wasn't angry with him, but I told him to keep them back. I don't want someone breathing down my back and I hope that you will do the same with your people. Philip winced and was glad that she couldn't see him. He had put an extra two men on her after her apartment was broken into. "Ok, Stasha, just don't put yourself out there for the pickings, ok."

Stasha reassured him that she would be careful and told him she loved him. "See you tomorrow." Hanging up the phone, Stasha went to climb into a hot bath. Relaxing in the hot water seemed to bring some relief to her sore muscles. Once the bath grew cool, Stasha dried herself off and went into the bedroom to put on some warm pajamas. Climbing into bed, she was out before her head hit the pillow.

The next morning, Stasha got up, but didn't feel any better. Getting dressed took some effort. She put a little make-up on to cover up how pale she was and did a lazy twist with her hair and put a clip in it. She was grateful that she had no meetings today. She knew that she would have to disappoint Philip tonight. She would tell him that she would take a rain check on dinner. Arriving at the office, Stasha realized that Tara wasn't at her desk. On her desk, Stasha saw a note from Tara. It said that she had to leave for a while and would be back after lunch. Stasha didn't mind if Tara had appointments to tend to. She always made sure that her work was done before taking a morning to do her appointments. She never left Stasha hanging.

The morning was productive and Stasha knew that she probably would have gotten more done if she didn't have this cold. Tara came back at lunch and took one look at Stasha and asked her if she would like her to get her some soup and a sandwich.

"Just the soup, thanks, Tara. I have no idea where I got this from but it's doing a number on me." Tara left and Stasha moved over to the couch. She just wanted to lay down for a moment. She heard Tara come back and sat up. "Thanks, this should help keep me going." Stasha relished the heat from the soup.

"I brought you some hot tea, too. You look like you could use it." Tara put it on the coffee table next to her soup.

"Why don't you go home if you don't feel so well?" Tara asked her.

"I want to get this paperwork finished and then I might be able to stay home tomorrow. Stasha finished the soup and brought the tea over to her desk with her.

"Could you do me a favor, Tara? Keep the teas coming?"

Tara nodded and told her if she could do anything to help her, just to buzz. As the afternoon wore on, Tara kept bringing the tea and Stasha started to feel a bit better. At four-thirty, Tara came into the office and asked her if she was going to finally head home.

"No, I'll probably stay for a while to finish this up. I have a meeting with this company on Monday and don't want to have to work this weekend. It will be easier if I just get it done. Thanks for asking."

Tara always made sure to come in and remind Stasha when it was four-thirty. Tom had insisted that she leave by five or five-thirty. This way, Stasha wouldn't get lost in work and stay late. Tara brought in another tea for her at about six o'clock and told her that she would be leaving. "Are you sure that you want to stay late?" Tara asked her.

"I'm almost done, and then I'm going to head out. See you on Monday. Have a good weekend." Stasha told her as Tara got ready to leave. Stasha sat at her desk and went through the rest of the reports. Taking a sip of her tea, she noticed that Tara must have used a different tea. It tasted sweeter than what she usually drank, but it was good. As another hour passed, Stasha finally gathered up her notes and the files and put them in her filing cabinet in her desk. Locking it, she decided to just lay on the couch until Philip arrived. If she fell asleep, he would wake her up. Everyone had packed up a half hour ago and the security guards had just made their rounds. Stasha laid down on the couch and realized that she was more tired than she thought. Closing her eyes, she fell asleep.

She was in the hallway and the feeling of panic was washing over her. She had to get out. Running down the hall, she knew that she had to get to the elevator before he caught her. "Why?" she kept asking herself as she ran; she trusted him at one time. All those years, she thought. As she reached the elevator, those arms came around her neck and held her. Stasha turned around and looked into a face she knew only to well.

Stasha sat up. She had the dream again, but this time she knew the person who had beaten her so badly. She had to phone the police. She needed Philip to be here. When she went to stand up, her legs felt like Jell-o. Stasha knew that she had to call someone. When she went to walk over to the phone, she turned and saw the person from her dream standing there with a grin on his face.

CHAPTER 18

Philip had just gotten into his car when his cell phone started to ring. Answering it, he thought it would be Stasha. "Hey babe, I should be there in about twenty minutes." Philip said.

"Hey, Philip, it's Brad. Did you just get off the plane?"

Philip told him that it just got in and that he was on his way to get Stasha at work.

"Philip, I think I know who our guy is and how he found out about the proceedings on the project that Stasha was working on. I was talking to Fran after she got home from work and she told me that Eric had asked her if she and Franny were still friends. Also, he asked her if Stasha was still trying to get the sorry-of-an-excuse project off the ground. Franny hated that guy and let slip that not only did she get it off the ground, but that it had already been sent out for government testing. Franny told me that she was sorry that she said anything, but he just made her so mad."

Philip wished that Franny hadn't said anything, but couldn't stop that now.

"Franny also told me that when she went to lunch at eleven, she saw Eric in the cafeteria and he wasn't alone. Tara was sitting there with him. Franny said that her mouth dropped when she saw her get up and give Eric a kiss before she left."

Philip couldn't believe what he was hearing. So that was how Eric knew how much progress was being done and why he wanted it stopped before it could take off. The only thing he didn't know was if it was completed. Stasha and Philip had moved it to his lab and Tara didn't work with them there. "Brad, I have to call Stasha and tell her I'm on my way." Philip didn't like the feeling that was starting to rise inside of him. Something didn't feel right. Dialing Stasha's private line at work, he let it ring and started to worry when she didn't pick up.

Stasha looked at Eric and noticed that he was not alone. Tara sat at Stasha's desk as if she owned it. "Eric, why did you do that to me three years ago?" Stasha tried to concentrate on him. She was still dizzy.

"Ah, I see that your memory has returned." Eric stood there with a twisted grin on his face. Tara came around the desk and went to stand next to Eric. Looking at Tara, Stasha said, "So that was how he got so much information. You must have fed him everything you could get your hands on. He must have trained you well. I'll let you in on a little secret, Tara, you see, the reason why we didn't stay together was because Eric wanted to train me to do his bidding, just like you're doing now. The only difference is, I'm more of a woman than you are and wouldn't let that happen," Stasha said.

Tara looked at Stasha with anger and yelled, "Your wrong, Stasha, Eric loves me."

Eric was getting pissed off at both of them. "Will you shut up, Tara. Do you really think that a man of my caliber would love a stupid girl like you? You played right into my hands. Did you ever wonder why I barely took you out? You were only good for two purposes, one was the valuable information you retrieved for me like a dog and the second was to have sex anytime I felt like it. By the way, you're not good at it, so don't make it a full time career."

Tara was in shock. All this time, he *had* used her. She gave up everything for him and this is how he treated her. Tara turned on him. Grabbing his hair, she screamed at him and scratched whatever part of his body she could get hold of.

Stasha knew that this was the perfect opportunity to get out of there. As Tara and Eric fought, Stasha rushed past them.

Eric saw her leave and knew that he couldn't let her get away. The bitch was going to ruin everything he had worked so hard for. If he couldn't get the copyright to this project, the people he dealt with wouldn't be too pleased. From what Franny said, it might already be over for him.

As Stasha ran down the hall, she looked back to see Eric grab Tara around the neck and twist it at an odd angle. Tara slumped to the floor. Eric started after Stasha. She had to get to the elevator. Stasha reached the elevator and pushed the button. Willing it to come, she was relieved when she heard the chime for her floor. Would she make it in time? Eric was almost to her. Just as the elevator opened, Eric was only a few feet from her.

"You've ruined me you bitch, you've ruined me."

As the elevator opened, Stasha looked into the eyes of the man she loved. Just as Eric made a jump to grab on to her, Philip yelled out. "Down now!" Stasha didn't need another second to think and threw herself on the floor. A loud roar ran through the corridor. Philip grabbed Stasha and helped her to her feet. Holding her against him, Philip knew that she was starting to cry. Looking back, Stasha realized that Philip shot Eric and killed him.

"He was going to kill me. Tara gave him everything that I had worked on." As Philip led Stasha downstairs, the police arrived and headed to the crime scene. "Honey, are you ok?"

At her nod, Philip told her how Brad had called and told him what Franny said. It all added up and he had called the police on his way. "He will never hurt anyone again," Philip told her and held her close.

CHAPTER 19

June 20, 1998

Standing in her room and looking out the window, Stasha could see how beautiful everything came together. There was a tent set up in the garden in the backyard, and flowers of every color. Monique and Jose had splendid ideas and the both of them made it all happen. Philip and Stasha wanted it to be a small wedding, but, with both fathers knowing so many people, it was not to be. Two hundred and fifty people would be attending. The meal to be served by the best catering company in Montreal would consist of filet minion, lobster tails, roasted chicken, baby potatoes, and asparagus in holidais sauce and caramelized baby carrots. Dessert was a simple vanilla ice cream with some cream de mint splashed on top. The bar was set up at the edge of the tent. While Stasha continued to watch, she could see some of the servers bringing Champaign around to the guests. They had decided that the guests would only have one glass before the ceremony.

Turning back to the mirror, Stasha looked at herself. Her hair was in a French twist with a few delicate tendrils falling down to soften her face. Her veil had a crown of pearls that nestled softly on top of her head. The gown she picked out was perfect. The straps were gathered silk that lay just off her shoulders and her bodice fit perfectly. It was made with Italian lace and silk, which enhanced the swells of her breast. Not too much showed. It also showed how tiny her waist really was. The skirt wasn't a full skirt, but lay softly against her legs. There was a small train, but it wouldn't be hampered by walking or dancing.

Franny and Lizabeth had just left to see if everything was ready for her. A knock came at the door and Stasha went across the room to open it.

Marcel looked at his daughter as she stood there in her wedding dress. Tears came into his eyes. Choked up, he said, "You look so beautiful. I can't believe that my little girl is getting married. I promised myself that I would be strong, but, honey, you remind me so much of your mother on our wedding day."

At this, Stasha grabbed a tissue and dabbed at her eyes. She wished that her mother could have been here. Monique tried to do everything right and Stasha was grateful, but she really wanted her own mother here for this special day.

Marcel reached into his breast pocket and pulled out an envelope. "Your mother made me promise her that on your wedding day I would give this to you. I will give you a few minutes alone and then I will be back."

As Marcel turned and closed the door behind him, Stasha stared down at the envelope he just placed in her hands. Walking over to the chair, Stasha sat down and opened it. There was a note inside.

My dearest, darling Stasha;

Today is your wedding day and I wanted you to know that I hope that from this day forward, all your dreams come true. I hope that you found a man that will stay true to you and love you. Remember, to make a marriage work, you must remain loyal to each other, as your father and I did for the time that we had together. Love to the fullest each and every day. I know that as you read this, you must be in your wedding dress. Please, my precious child, do not cry. I want you to know that I am always with you and, even though I'm not there in body, I am in your heart, and there is where I will remain. As the sun shines, you will know that I will be looking down upon you this very day with all my love.

Love Mom

Marcel walked back in and stood at the door and watched how his daughter cried for a woman who loved them both. He knew that

Marie-Claire would have been so proud of her. Walking up to Stasha, he held her in his arms and told her that everything would be fine. "Your mother wanted me to give you something on this day." Opening the box, he took out a gold locket and stepped around Stasha so he could secure it around her neck.

Stasha looked down and opened the locket. There was a picture of her and her mother. Marie-Claire, with her long blond hair and the eyes Stasha saw everyday when she looked into the mirror. Stasha sat on her lap with the blue velvet dress and her hair in ribbons. Both smiled for the camera.

"Your mother left a note for me and told me that I was to give this to you on your wedding day, too. She told me that a bride needed something old, which would be the locket. I've kept it these many years for you, but, what I don't understand is, she said something about something blue. I'm sorry, but nothing blue was left with it."

Stasha could feel the tears begin to form once more in her eyes. "Daddy, she did leave me something blue. Mom bought me the dress in the photo. See Daddy, its blue." Drying the tears from their eyes, they proceed to the garden. Walking outside, Stasha wished that the clouds would go away just for today. The music started. As she walked down the isle towards Philip, who stood there waiting at the alter, Stasha smiled. Marcel kissed her cheek and then handed her to the husband to be. As they joined hands, Stasha looked up and noticed the sun breaking through the clouds and shining down on all of them. Looking up into Philip's eyes, Stasha knew that all the dreams she ever had would come true.

423639

Made in the USA